A COWGIRL'S PRIDE

BARRELS AND HEARTS SERIES BOOK 4

EDITH MACKENZIE

This is a work of fiction. Names, **characters**, businesses, places, events, locales, and incidents are either the products of the author's imagination or used in a fictitious manner. Any resemblance to actual persons, living or dead, or actual events is purely coincidental

A Cowgirl's Passion (Barrels & Hearts #3):

Images © DepositPhotos – Geridbody & Alan Poulson Cover Design © Designed with Grace

Created with Vellum

❉ Created with Vellum

To all the misunderstood cowgirls out there, doing it tough and trying their best. I see you.

She had been in a lot of places in her life, especially in those dark years of her adolescence, but never anything like this. The acidic smell of freshly painted walls, having only been completed the day before, mingled with the mellow aroma of rubber floor tiles that covered the outside aisle and stalls as Megan stepped into the laboratory with the rest of the girls. Everywhere she cast her gaze was a marvel, her senses sent into overdrive. The recently fitted stainless-steel counters still had their protective plastic adhered to them, a microscope sitting on a bench, pride of place, underneath overhead shelving laden with slides, specimen jars and other apparatuses that Megan wasn't familiar with. Swiveling around, she found a sterilization unit, fridge and computer.

"Bloody heck," Deb said in amazed approval. "I can't even process how awesome this all is."

"As the person footing the bill, I can tell you, no expense was spared," Frankie added, smiling with satisfaction at the veterinarian perfection set before her. "But even I am impressed, Gabi."

Gabi nodded graciously, accepting their approval. "Next on our tour is the mare and foal crush, followed by the operating theater."

"Say what?" Megan asked, unsure if she had heard correctly.

"The mare and foal crush?" Gabi repeated.

"No, the other one. Are you saying that we actually have a purpose-built equine operating theater onsite?"

Gabi smirked. "Yep, and the only privately owned one—in any barrel racing ranch that I know of, at least."

Megan shook her head in amazement. She seriously had to give it to that girl—she dreamed big and usually got her way. *But she's one of those golden people,* the little voice in her head niggled, always finding the negative. *Not like me.*

Sullenly, she waited while the others trooped from the lab, meaning to join on the end. As she closed the door behind her, she spied a staircase set against one wall. Remembering that the vet barn included accommodation, she decided to investigate, conscious that this might be her only chance to check it out before Carlos moved in. Her soft footfalls barely made any noise as she traipsed up, the unlocked door only further justifying her decision. The new hinges gave a little squeak of protest as the door smoothly swung open. *Gabi might want to get someone to look at that,* she thought as she peeked in.

Inside, a yellow sofa was barely visible, surrounded by stacks of boxes, a man's shirt carelessly thrown over the top of one. She did a double take. That didn't seem right. She stepped further into the room as she focused on the garment. The sharp brightness of someone turning on the light made Megan's stomach drop in fright.

"What the bloody heck?" she uttered in surprise.

"I could say the same thing, but probably not with such an Australian flavor," a warmly amused, if somewhat sleepy, masculine voice replied. Megan traced the source of the voice to find a shirtless, tousled-haired Carlos lounging against what she could only assume was the bedroom door.

"But no one is meant to be here." Uncomfortably off kilter, her usual swagger fled faster than a gambler from a bookie.

"Well, obviously, I didn't get Gabi's memo," he fired back, still looking like he could feature in a hot guys calendar.

"What memo didn't you get?" Gabi's voice floated up from the stairs. Judging by the sounds, she and the rest of the girls were on their way up.

Frustration left a sour taste in Megan's mouth. *Of course, wasn't it always the way that everyone shows up right when she had made a meal of things? Next, Deb will be making some sort of wisecrack.*

"I see Megan has already sniffed out the hot guy." Deb entered the room close on Gabi's heels. "And he doesn't even have a shirt on. Nice work, Megan." She winked at Megan in approval.

"I didn't know he was here," Megan ground out.

"Actually, why are you here?" Gabi asked Carlos, a brow raised suspiciously. "Weren't you meant to be arriving at the end of the month?"

Carlos didn't meet his sister's eyes as he gathered up his earlier discarded shirt. "Well, I tied up loose ends in Kentucky earlier than I expected and thought I would take the opportunity to start unpacking my things and get settled in." Megan watched his glorious abs vanish from view, covered by his snug fitting shirt. A quick glance showed that, except for Gabi, everyone else was also somewhat saddened by the disappearing act.

"What loose ends?" Gabi pushed, undeterred by her brother's dissembling.

"You know, this and that." Carlos scratched his head with

a sniff. "I have to give you credit, sis, you did a good job building this. In fact, I was having a top-class nap in the bedroom before the gorgeous Megan interrupted me." He sent her a flirty wink. "She can wake me up anytime."

"For Pete's sake, don't tell her that. You'll never get any sleep again," Deb fired back. Megan shot her a dirty look, promising violence if she didn't keep her mouth shut.

Intercepting the look, Frankie took pity on Megan. "I think we still have a few more things that Gabi needs to show us."

But isn't that always the way—Frankie playing peacekeeper? Megan's mind whispered.

Gabi skewered her brother with a hard look. "Don't think this conversation is over."

"I was never in any doubt. I'm sure you will pick it up at your earliest convenience, which will probably be tomorrow when you corner me as I visit Joao," he replied urbanely.

As everyone left, Carlos called out. "I meant what I said, pretty Megan."

MEGAN WATCHED as Gabi took her usual place at the kitchen table. She had to give it to her, the girl walked in like she was entering a boardroom. Amused, Megan looked around at her friends, trying to picture them in corporate attire. Gabi, obviously, would be the driven CEO, Frankie the high-flying executive, Chloe the young, eager intern, Deb—

"Megan, are you okay with that?" Gabi's voice broke through her imaginings.

"Yeah, not gonna lie, I kinda spaced out there," she admitted with a shrug. Chloe let out a giggle that earned her an unimpressed glare from Gabi.

"I need everyone to focus," Gabi continued, sweeping an

exasperated glance across the group. "Things are about to get next level crazy around here and everyone—" She stopped to spear Megan with a glance, which Megan thought was a little unfair. She was pretty certain most of the others daydreamed in Gabi's endless meetings as well. "And I mean *everyone* needs to stay on task." Pausing to gather her thoughts, Gabi looked down at her notes. "Megan, I was saying that, as the stud manager, you're coming into a busy time with foaling season about to start. I want you to make sure that we have everything we could possibly need on hand to cope with anything that might come our way." Megan bit down, silencing her scathing reply that this wasn't her first rodeo and she was, in fact, an incredibly experienced stud manager. Instead, she gave a little nod. "Once Carlos has settled in, let's make a standing weekly appointment for him to check the mares."

"I'll add it to my schedule," Megan noted, relieved when Gabi had already shifted her attention to Chloe.

"Chloe, we have less horses in work now that we have closed our training books. After you finish riding each day, I'll need you to float between Deb and Megan and help with whatever they need." Finally, the help that she'd been promised, for what, two years now?

Chloe bounced excitedly. "Whatever you need me to do, Gabi." Megan rolled her eyes. She liked the girl, but did she have to suck up so much?

"Deb, are we on top of everything? Anything I need to know? No? Okay." Gabi shifted her focus to Frankie. Megan narrowed her eyes. How on earth did Deb escape so easily?

"Frankie, the first clinic is rapidly approaching. That reminds me, I need to get the arena surface topped up. Deb, can you start getting the mares in the paddocks closest to the arena moved to the new paddocks? Also, start getting those areas cleaned up. We'll need to get traffic cones and organize porta-toilets. We still have time, but as this is our first one, I think we're bound to forget something. Chloe, I want you to be Frankie's assistant for the clinic as she's on the road a lot leading up to it. On the actual weekend, everyone will be busy, and she'll need a hand. Vegas is looking good for you this year, Frankie."

"It better be looking good. This is my bloody year to go," Megan said. "Especially since I missed getting to see you win the bloody American. No pressure, but I'm going to need you to win Vegas to make up for it."

Frankie laughed at her friend's enthusiasm. "No pressure at all. I'll see what I can do." She gave Megan a wink.

"Just to finish up, I know we have a lot on our plates, but I thought, since we're going to have a good sized crowd here for the clinic, we might as well host the grand opening of the vet barn on the Saturday night." Gabi looked around the table, trying to gauge reactions to her idea. She looked a little surprised when Megan nodded eagerly.

"I think it's perfect timing. Credit where credit is bloody due. You did a great job with the vet barn and I, for one, can't wait to see it put to use," Megan declared.

"Or put someone to use. Maybe a certain Brazilian vet?" Deb wiggled her eyebrows at her friend.

"As stud manager, Deb, if I have to take one for the team, then that's a sacrifice I'm willing to make."

CHAPTER 2

Carlos poked his head into the room, relief evident when he saw his sister busy studying various samples and swatches with a chicly dressed woman. He gave an approving glance at the woman he assumed was Gabi's interior designer, his eyes showing his appreciation of a beautiful woman. Gabi, spying him, excused herself from Jade. "Stop that!" Gabi said sharply, tapping him on the nose like a wayward puppy.

He blinked in surprise at the action, jerking his head back. "Gabi, a beautiful woman is something that a man should take the time to admire. She is like art. A delight to the senses. It would be criminal not to respond to her charm." Jade blushed under his regard, a little giggle escaping her.

Gabi was not amused by his explanation, nor her designer's schoolgirl response. "Do not leave before I talk to you. I want answers, Carlos," she commanded.

Extracting himself from Gabi's clutches, he retreated from the room and went in search of Joao. He found his friend in the barn, admiring his new tractor. "That's an impressive piece of equipment, and I'm not talking about the owner," he congratulated.

Joao beamed at him. "It is, isn't it?" He looked closely at Carlos. "You look remarkably intact for having come from the house. Did Gabi not see you?" Realization dawned on him. "She was too busy with the designer, wasn't she? Smart man."

Carlos absentmindedly rubbed his nose. "Maybe not completely unscathed. She did not like me sweet talking the pretty little designer."

Joao laughed. "You are still charming the birds from the trees with your silver tongue. Are you going to tell me why you have come back early? I would have thought you would not be so eager to leave your fancy girlfriend in Kentucky."

Carlos stared at the tractor, his expression clouding. "She broke up with me."

Joao cleared his throat, busying himself at the base of the tractor. "That is rough. I thought you were solid."

"So did I. I didn't see it coming," he admitted, eyes downcast. "But you know, she was pretty high maintenance. I have a lot more time and money now that we aren't together." He looked back at the tractor. "The Black Angus gig must be paying all right if you can afford this fancy rig."

"Can't complain."

THE DUST BILLOWED SOFTLY, the cloud trailing the truck as it made its way down the drive, silhouetted by the brilliant colors of the setting sun. Carlos had timed his escape well. Having seen Gabi farewell her designer, he knew his sister too well and wasn't willing to risk an interrogation at her hands. He glanced in the rearview mirror to see her make her way over to the barn. He laughed as he saw her scrunched her face up in frustration at the sight of his departure. He didn't know how Joao put up with her. As he watched his best friend laugh fondly and put his arm around Gabi, he could only imagine what was being said between them, but whatever it was made his ears burn. The last thing he glimpsed as he headed for the road was Joao leading his irate wife back into the house.

~

ON THE NEIGHBORING RANCH, Megan and Chloe watched Delila and Nova framed against the same backdrop of glorious colors. Megan rested her foot against the bottom rail of the fence, drinking in the peaceful splendor that came from this hour of the day. Her soul was briefly at ease with the world.

"I can't wait for the foals to start arriving. Nova was so cute when she was little, but a whole herd at the same time?" Chloe clutched her hands to her heart. "I don't think I will be able to handle the cuteness."

"It was always my favorite time of the year at the stud back home," Megan admitted, resting her chin on her hands. "But it's a lot of stress. So many things can go wrong. It breaks your heart when you lose a foal or mare or, worse, both."

"I didn't even really think about what happens when things go wrong."

"Chloe, something to remember on a farm or ranch is that, if you work with livestock, you will, at some point, deal with deadstock. All we can do is minimize the risks." She gave the suddenly somber girl a reassuring smile. "Anyway, we have a vet onsite, and Gabi says Carlos is really experienced and qualified."

"And cute." Chloe giggled.

"I'm sure the mares will appreciate that." Megan's eyes returned to the pair of horses. "For all the worry and hard work, it's worth it. I've always loved working with foals and their mamas."

CHAPTER 3

The latch clicked into place, securing the horse safely in the vet crush. Megan craned her neck around to watch from her position at the horse's head as Carlos began his examination on the last mare. "Okay, Missy, just a quick check of temperature to begin with," he crooned to the animal. In response, Missy agitatedly swished her tail, giving him a stinging flick to the face. "Easy, Missy, didn't mean anything personal, but all the other lovely ladies let me take their temps without too much protest."

"This one wants to be wined and dined first." Megan snorted, enjoying the mare's antics. She liked seeing the usually-in-control vet on the back foot. "I'd say she's telling you that you're moving too fast."

Carlos stepped away from the mare, raising a lazy brow at Megan. "It appears I have a critic to my wooing style." He walked to the head of the offended Missy and gave her neck a stroke. Megan was mesmerized watching his hand move against the hide of the horse in slow, firm strokes, a warmth blooming in her chest. Seriously, she needed to stop reading so many romance novels.

"Now, Missy, darling, I am going to have a listen to your heart and then see if we can hear anything from that wiggly little baby you have in your belly," he said in dulcet tones while his hand remained in motion. He gave a satisfied little nod as he held the stethoscope to her side, just behind her foreleg at first, then moving further along her flank. "Very good, pretty mama," he murmured encouragingly. He resumed his position to the rear of the crush, his hand resting gently on the horse's hindquarters. "Missy, me darlin', all we have to do is try to check your temperature again and you're all done for the day." This time, the mare didn't protest and Carlos, looking pleased with himself, completed his examination, giving Missy a pat. "She's all good to be returned to the paddock."

Megan unlatched the front gate and led the mare out of the confines of the crush. "Here I was thinking I was going to have to stand here all day as you sweet talked her," she said, heading toward the barn's exit.

"Well, apparently my first approach was too fast and now you say I took too long." He wiped his sweaty brow with the back of his hand. "It's very hard to please you." He sent her a flirty wink.

"You won't know till you try," she threw over her shoulder, laughing.

"Is that a challenge, Megan?"

Surprised he'd responded to her teasing, she was grateful her back was to him and he couldn't see the heightened color in her face. She pretended she was too far away to hear and hurried the mare toward her paddock.

THE GENTLE ROLLING of the tractor as it slashed the tall grass and weeds lulled Megan into allowing her mind to roam.

With only a week to go before Frankie's first clinic, it was all hands on deck to get the ranch presentable before the masses arrived. A secret smile danced across her lips, her pale green eyes sparkling merrily as Megan thought back to Carlos's teasing. It had been nice to be flirted with by a cute guy, especially one who had the macho appeal of the dark-haired vet. If she was honest with herself, for all the reputation her friends tried to bestow upon her, she was rarely on the receiving end of male attention.

Megan shifted in her seat at the controls of the tractor, her face beginning to feel warm as she thought about Carlos, of his sexy winks and strong, soothing hands. Turning the corner of the field, she straightened and headed the machine back toward the barn. In the distance, she could see Carlos's truck pulling up and him waving. She returned his greeting, a flutter forming in her belly at seeing him again, only to notice Chloe walking from the barn, who was very obviously the target of the gesture.

The butterflies that had danced about excitedly only moments before fell like little lead balls in the pit of her stomach. *A guy like that? Of course a guy like that would chase the pretty young blonde. They always did, not the—*she looked down at herself—*not someone like me.* Staring straight ahead, she glumly drove the tractor back to the machinery shed.

THE SCRAPE of the shovel against the concrete floor provided the soundtrack to Megan's sour thoughts as she prepared the buckets in the feed room. Retrieving a scoop of grain from the barrel, she turned, slamming hard into Chloe. The grain sprayed through the air, spilling on the floor. "Bloody heck, Chloe!"

"Gosh, I'm sorry, Megs." Chloe dropped to her knees and started picking up the spilled fodder.

Chaff sticking to her sweaty neck and sweat trickling down her face, Megan glared at Chloe. "Leave it."

"I can clean it up."

"I said leave it!" Jealous anger poured through her, no longer able to be held at bay.

Chloe awkwardly rose to her feet, uncertainty written across her face. "Megan...?"

"Darn it, Chloe, you're always in the way. Every time I turn around, you're there. When I wake up, when I try and do my work, heck, when I eat my dinner. You're always there and you're always in the way. I'm sick of it. Why don't you just leave me alone?"

Chloe's eyes filled with tears, her bottom lip quivering as she stared at Megan with hurt-filled eyes before bolting from the room. "Chloe, I didn't—" But it was too late, the girl had already fled. Megan was flooded with regret, feeling like she'd just kicked a puppy.

"I hope you're bloody proud of yourself." Deb loomed angrily in the door.

"Look, I didn't mean it," Megan said, sweeping up the feed.

"I don't give two bloody hoots if you meant it or not. The fact is you bloody well said it—and to one of the nicest people going around. That girl looked like her heart had been broken when she rushed past me."

Megan stopped sweeping. "I'll find her later and say sorry, okay?"

Deb glared at her, in no way mollified by Megan's offer of an apology. "You bloody better. But what I want to know is why you always revert back to being such a bloody cow." Without another word, she turned her back on Megan and left.

CHAPTER 4

Megan ran, her running shoes kissing the land, the gravel of the dirt road crunching underfoot. The warm humidity made her feel sticky. Her clothes and hair, slick with perspiration, clung to her skin. Sweat rolled down her body in thick, salty beads. She could feel her heart throbbing in her chest. Running was something that Megan had always done. There was something about being alone in the still of the early morning that helped her cope with life. And life had been tough for her—the scars of childhood still plagued her now. She had never been good enough, always being made to feel like she was inferior. *That's why I'm alone now,* her insecurities whispered to her. *And always will be. Deb was right, I'm a cow. Being alone is what I deserve.*

Remorse suffocated her as surely as the stuffy air, the sting of Deb's rebuttal still smarting. She didn't know why she'd been so horrible to Chloe. She actually thought she was a sweet girl. But seeing Carlos fall over himself the other day... Well, it had made her want to lash out. It wasn't fair that, once again, the hot guy was passing her over for the cute, young blonde. *Why wouldn't he be interested in Chloe?* her mind mocked. *Compared to plain, dumpy me, why wouldn't he choose her?*

Megan tried to ignore the thoughts that fought and twisted in her brain. She could still see Chloe's hurt face as she had fled. Poor kid didn't deserve to be yelled at, she'd only been trying to help. But now she probably thought Megan was a cow, too. She turned and began the long run back to the ranch, wondering if maybe it might have been a better idea to just keep running into the distance.

Megan rushed from the room, almost knocking Frankie over in her haste to exit. Frankie looked around at the occupants of the room. "Was it something I said?"

"No, I think it's me," Chloe said sadly, her face a picture of dejection. "I don't think she likes me very much anymore. I'm not entirely sure what I've done to make her hate me."

Deb gave a mirthless laugh. "That's our Megan for you. Seriously, I wouldn't stress about it. She's a bloody moody little thing at the best of times. There was a time not so long ago when she was being a cow to me, too. Turns out she was bloody jealous." Deb fastened a speculative eye on Chloe. "Have you stolen a man from her?"

Chloe's eye's opened wide in horrified denial. "I would never do that!"

Frankie gave Deb a little nudge. "Leave her alone."

"Which one?" Deb countered.

"Both of them. Chloe, she's just teasing and Megan, well, Megan can be a bit…" Frankie searched for the right word. "Prickly, at times. But she really does have a heart of gold. You need to understand that things haven't always been easy for her. She's had to look out for herself and that makes it hard for her to let someone in and means she's always on the defensive."

Chloe nodded dubiously. "Well, as long as you think I haven't done anything wrong..." She trailed off.

"I guarantee it. And honestly, she'll get her panties out of a bunch soon enough and it'll all blow over. Speaking of which, I wish this clinic was all over." Frankie moaned, resting her head pitifully on the table.

"That bad?" Deb asked solicitously, handing her the cookie jar.

Frankie reached her hand in and extracted a choc chip cookie. "Gabi assures me everything is organized and going to schedule, but that's easy for her to say. She doesn't have to stand up there in front of everyone and talk for Two. Whole. Days." She shoved the whole cookie in her mouth dramatically.

"But you're never quiet," joked Deb.

"Frank oww eerie uch," mumbled Frankie, crumbs falling from her mouth.

Deb cupped a hand to her ear. "Once again, and this time in English, please."

Frankie swallowed noisily. "Ha ha, you're so funny. I said thank you very much. But what happens if I freeze or they think I don't know what I'm talking about?"

"Um, you're the current American Rodeo Champion, which you won as a qualifier no less, and are sitting in the number three spot on the leadership ladder for world champ and have earned your place for Vegas. I'm pretty sure you know what you're talking about," Chloe offered, sneaking a cookie. "Anyway, you have me as an assistant. Just blame me if anything goes wrong."

Frankie looked horrified. "I could never."

Deb looked impressed. "I don't know, I kinda like how this kid thinks."

"Well I think it's going to be great." Chloe reached for the jar again. "Does anyone mind if I have the last one?"

~

THE STALLS of the vet barn were still spotlessly clean, straw bales sitting in neat stacks in front of each one, ready to be used when required. Megan would have noticed the piles if she hadn't been locked in self-loathing, shoulder's hunched and head bowed low. As it was, she didn't see them and proceeded to ram her shin into the spikey edge of one just before she made it to the lab door.

"What the?" she bit out. Glaring at the offending bale, eyes narrowed, she lined it up and kicked it with all of her might. Feeling strangely vindicated for the action, she proceeded to repeat it until her emotional well ran dry. Giving a satisfied nod, she bent to brush off her jeans.

"Remind me not to make you angry." A darkly rich, masculine voice chuckled from behind her.

Jerking in surprise, she straightened up. Dread trickled through her at the thought of exactly who to expect as she turned around. "Have you been standing there long?"

"Long enough to see you put that straw firmly back in its place. The only question I have is what did it do to deserve that kind of beating?"

Megan hated how her belly fluttered just by looking at his darkly handsome face. "It knows what it did." She wiped her sweaty palms discretely on her jeans. "Gabi said it was okay for me to get some supplies to restock our kits before the clinic."

"What my sister wants, she usually gets." Carlos turned toward the lab door, unlatching it, gesturing for her to precede him. "Do you have a list, or is this more in the nature of a general raiding party?"

"I know exactly what I want."

"I bet you do." A soft smirk of mischief was softened by the dancing dimples that appeared in both cheeks.

Megan pulled a crumpled piece of paper from her pocket, ignoring the tingle deep and low in her belly that his smile caused. "I brought a shopping list."

"I prefer to make it up as I go. It's more exciting that way." Carlos switched on the lights. "Some light, so I can see your pretty smile as you shop."

Megan smiled despite herself. "My gosh, do you ever bloody stop flirting?"

His brow crinkled as he tilted his head. "But where's the fun in that? Life is too short to be taken seriously all of the time."

"So, you're never serious when you flirt?" She found herself speaking before she could stop the words tumbling out.

His eyes darkened, kicking her heartbeat into overdrive. "I didn't say that."

The hope she had been feeling that maybe the flirtation she had seen between him and Chloe was nothing more than harmless fun fled before his words. "Oh."

As if reading her mind, he stepped closer. "I didn't see you the other day after you parked up the tractor. I waited for a bit, but you'd disappeared."

"Yeah, I mean you looked busy and I had lots of things I had to do, you know, with the clinic."

He laughed again, white teeth flashing. "Boy, do I know it. Gabi's whipping everyone and everything into tiptop shape for this clinic. She even has me giving a talk about rehab for injured sport horses."

Megan placed the last roll of bandaging into her bag. "I think I have everything I need. I'd better get back before Gabi decides I've fallen behind on her schedule." Ducking her head, she hastened toward the door, chasing the safety of not being in a room with the man that caused her emotions to chase and tumble over themselves.

"Megan?"

One more stride and she would be outside. "Yeah?"

"You should smile more. Your whole face lights up when you do. It's beautiful."

Not trusting herself to respond, she legged it, not daring to look back.

CHAPTER 5

The sun glinted off the rows of neatly parked horse trailers, a metallic patchwork of all size and monetary investment. Frankie's face went pale as she gawked out from the barn. Without warning, she spun on her heel and dashed back toward the bunkhouse, her hand pressed tightly against her mouth.

"Oh, crap," Deb muttered, appraising the situation. "Chloe, Megan, you guys better stay with Frankie, I think this is something for Gabi to bloody well deal with."

Chloe trailed up the stairs behind Megan, hesitantly standing as far as humanly possible away from the other woman. Megan rolled her eyes. She didn't have time to deal with her antics when she need to focus on what was going on the other side of the bathroom door. "Ah, Frankie? Are you okay? Do you need me to do something?"

The sound of vomit spluttering into the toilet echoed violently within. A watery cough was followed by weak sniffling. "I just need a moment," Frankie wanly replied. The toilet flushed and she staggered from the bathroom, gratefully accepting the glass of water Chloe held out for her. Megan was surprised the girl had shown the initiative to get it unasked. "You'd think I'd be better at handling my nerves by now," Frankie said.

"You get nervous?" Chloe asked in surprise.

"Don't look so shocked. Of course I do."

"But, but you're Frankie Navarro. You're famous!" spluttered Chloe.

"Who's famous?" asked Gabi marching into the room, Deb trotting at her heels.

"Frankie is."

"I wouldn't go that far," Deb said. "We try to keep her humble. Can you imagine the ego if we let her actually believe her own press? Next thing you know, she'll want to star in her own movie."

Gabi squinted speculatively at Frankie. "I like the sound of a movie. I wonder who you need to talk with to make that happen." Megan could almost hear the cogs in her brain turning, in fact she would bet money on the fact that, as soon as she had a quiet moment, Gabi was probably going to pursue the idea. Gabi looked intently at her ashen friend. "What happened?"

"The usual. I knew there were a few people coming for the weekend, but when I saw all of those trailers lined up, well, there was a lot." Frankie let out a nervous laugh.

"Yes, and they're all here to see you," Chloe said encouragingly, her face glowing with anticipation. "It's so exciting!" Frankie groaned weakly.

Deb shook her head warningly at the younger woman. "I don't think that's helping, Chloe."

Gabi took Frankie's shoulders firmly. "You need to buck up, Frankie. You're very good at what you do. You are a talented rider and an even more amazing trainer and horsewoman. Just do what comes naturally, and you will be fine."

"That was actually a pretty good pep talk," Deb congratulated Gabi.

"Thank you," Gabi said humbly as she assessed Frankie. "Are you going to be able to do this?"

Frankie nodded. "I just need to start and then I'll be all right. It's just, well, I need to get past the nerves to start."

"Chloe," Deb said.

"Yeah?"

"Looks like you have a new task as part of being Frankie's assistant."

"What's that?"

"Chief bucket holder."

~

IT HADN'T BEEN EASY, but Megan had managed to juggle doing the jobs assigned to her for the clinic and avoid the others at the same time. Knowing how anxious Frankie could get in high pressure situations, she'd been absurdly proud of her friend as she had grown in confidence over the course of the day. Watching her working with the riders and their horses, seeing the improvement as each left the arena, she knew the weekend was going to be a huge success. Another in a long line for Frankie.

Feeling unworthy, she headed to the vet barn and finished setting up the chairs, grateful she had timed it with Carlos having lunch at his parents' house. The serenity she usually felt at being alone eluded her, despondency turning her features sad. Instead of feeling tranquil in the peace and quiet, she instead felt like a pariah, picturing her friends, enjoying themselves in her absence.

"So, this is where you're hiding." Mitch's voice interrupted her maudlin thoughts.

"I'm working, Mitch. Do you see anyone else up here

getting this ready?" she threw over her shoulder as she moved another chair into place.

"I might be wrong about this, but I don't think I am. What's really going on, Megs?" He sat down on one of her recently positioned chairs. "Sit down and talk to me."

Megan weighed her options in her mind before deciding to ungraciously plonk down beside him. "What do you want to talk about? I assume you came here with something in mind. Deb has probably filled you in on most of it."

Mitch winced under the sharp edge of her words. "Yeah, she's told me some, but I also live in the same house as you and Chloe. And I'd like to think that I'm your mate, too. I know you're unhappy, and I thought that maybe you might want to talk it over with me. Just get it off your bloody chest."

"I didn't appreciate it when Deb called me a bloody cow."

"Fair enough."

"Everyone acts like it's just a thing—*oh, Megan's being a cow again*. And not once has anyone stopped and asked me what happened to make me act that way," she blurted out bitterly.

"What happened to make you act that way, then?" There was something to the non-judgmental way he asked that cracked her hard shell.

"I don't mean to do it. I just can't help it. Especially after seeing her and…" Megan looked down at her fingers, tightly locked together. "What's wrong with me, Mitch? Why didn't you like me?"

"I do bloody like you," he objected sharply. "And I've never bloody thought there was anything wrong with you."

"Not like that. Back before you and Deb." Megan cringed at the vulnerability in her voice. "I'm so lonely." She gave a sad little smile. "How dumb is that? I'm surrounded by friends and I'm so bloody lonely. I'm always the one that gets passed over. Frankie has the talent, Deb is Miss Personality, Gabi is, like, super businesswoman. They all have their men. And to make it worse? Now there's cute, perky Chloe that has men throwing themselves at her. What do I have? Nothing."

Mitch blinked at the loathing in her voice, clearly surprised at what had been festering beneath the surface. "Megan, there's nothing wrong with you."

"So why didn't you pick me? Why doesn't anyone ever pick me?"

Mitch took her hand in his. She looked away, unable to bare the pity that she saw reflected in his expression. "Megan," he began gently. "There's nothing wrong with you. It was just that my heart knew that it wanted Deb."

"And Frankie?" she asked bitterly. "Your heart wanted Frankie, too?"

He coughed awkwardly. "Frankie was an infatuation."

"But still, I wasn't the one that you chose. I'm never the one chosen. Just some sloppy reject left in the corner."

"Megan, I need you to listen to what I'm going to say, and I mean really bloody listen. Hear what I'm saying. This resentment"—Mitch gestured at her vaguely—"you need to let it go. It's taking a toll on your happiness, your ability to enjoy life and your mates. Just let it all go and reclaim some control instead of striking out at everyone all the bloody time. Don't you find it tiring?"

"You—"

"No, Megan, I don't have anything else to say. Well, that's not true. I love you, and your mates love you, and you need to decide to let yourself be worthy of that." He stood, gave her a gentle kiss on the head and ambled away.

Megan's gaze bore into his departing back, his words

rankling as she twisted and turned them in her mind. A sliver of guilt wormed its way into her heart, recognizing the truth that he had spoken, no matter how hard it had been to hear. Recognizing it was one thing, but acting on it? Well, that was something else entirely. For once, her inner demon was silent.

CHAPTER 6

"It looks good, doesn't it?"

Megan stopped near the barn door and looked in the direction of Gabi's excited voice. Gabi, pride etched on her features, looked around in satisfaction and Megan followed her gaze. It was true. The vet barn was a marvel in cutting edge broodmare and equine veterinary facilities. A wide band of Brazilian green ribbon was strung across the barn entryway, waiting to be cut.

"You did well, Gabriella. It is spectacular," Joao said approvingly, his arm draped across her shoulders. He smiled in greeting at the tall, lanky man heading toward them, a small girl at his side, two identical young women trailing behind him. "Hello, Travis. Did you get dragged to this opening, too?" Joao said, shaking hands firmly with him.

Travis gave a wry smile. "No, I'm here with my nieces, Ash"—he gestured to one of the auburn-haired girls—"and this is Savannah. He tousled Teeny's hair, setting her to giggling. "And I think you remember this little munchkin."

"How did you enjoy the first day?" Gabi, all business, enquired of the twins.

"I think my brain hurts," Ash responded, emerald green eyes dramatically wide.

She was interrupted by Teeny's loud cry of "Chloe!" before the little girl dashed toward the young woman.

Chloe picked the exuberant girl up, laughing. "Teeny, where have you been hiding?" she asked, walking back toward the group.

"Daddy and I have been helping my cousins. They want to be as good as Frankie, but no one is as good as Frankie. Frankie is the best." The words tumbled out, knocking into each other as Teeny gazed adoringly up at Chloe.

"Hello, everyone," Chloe said, glancing curiously at the newcomers, before blushing slightly when she looked at Travis. Introductions were made quickly. Teeny, growing impatient to get Chloe's attention returned to her, tugged on her friend's hand. "Yes, Teeny?"

"Can we go see Nova?"

"Now, Teeny, Chloe has been working all day. She probably just wants to sit down and relax." Travis smiled apologetically.

Chloe's blush deepened under his regard. "It's not a bother. I can take her over for a bit and then be back before the ribbon is cut."

"Is it okay if we come, too?" asked Savannah. "I'd love to see Delila's foal. She was the first horse we saw Frankie race on."

"Do you think we could see Sampson, too?" Ash added, her eyes wide at the prospect.

Chloe flicked a glance at Gabi for approval. "I don't think that would be a problem," Gabi said. "Just make sure you're back before we start the opening."

"We will," the three older girls promised simultaneously, before all of them broke out in giggles at the coincidence. "Jinx," they all shrieked, before more eruptions of mirth.

Megan, standing as she was, if not fully hidden, at least partially concealed by the shadows within the barn, watched the scene before her. Her hand cupped her mouth. *How could she be so stupid?* she mentally berated herself. All of that energy wasted on being jealous and it was pretty obvious the girl had a major crush on Travis. *I guess every girl goes through a stage of having a thing for the older man.* Megan cast her eyes heavenward. *Guess this means I really do owe her an apology.*

"WITH THE COMPLETION of this facility, I feel confident that no other ranch can provide the level of care to visiting horses and broodmares that Affinity Ranch can. This addition would not be possible without the generous support of our business partner, Need for Speed Champion, American Champion and, God willing, the next World Champion—our very own Frankie Navarro and her husband Luciano." Gabi waited for the applause to die down. "It gives me great honor to officially open the Ana and Eduardo Equine Veterinarian Facility." And without further ado, she proficiently cut the ribbon.

"You never told us what you were planning on calling it!" Sra Ana cried in humble astonishment. Carlos was proud of his kid sister having decided on the name. Their parents had done so much for both of them.

"Well, we discussed it amongst ourselves, and we couldn't think of anyone we would like to name it after more," Frankie said, wrapping the overwrought woman in her arms. "You know we all love you and Senhor Eduardo."

"Personally, I wanted to name it the Carlos Care Facility, but I was outvoted." Carlos laughed, gesturing as if the name was in lights. He was only half joking. Honestly, his name would look great in lights.

Gabi punched him in the arm. "That was never going to happen."

"Chloe, is it okay if I talk to you for a moment?" Megan asked quietly. Chloe looked surprised to be singled out, surprised and apprehensive.

"Should we be worried for her safety?" Deb asked bluntly, giving Megan a hard look.

Megan shook her head, smiling ruefully. "No, not anymore."

As the two women left to seek somewhere more private for their discussion, Carlos looked around curiously. "Did I miss something?"

"Yes, you did," Gabi replied tartly. "And before you ask, it's none of your business."

$$\sim$$

MEGAN COULD SEE Chloe's mouth working, her fingers restlessly picking at her cuticle as she watched Megan apprehensively. Clearly, she was uncertain what Megan wished to speak about, probably dreading that it would involve her getting another telling off. Guilt slammed into Megan's gut, momentarily robbing her of breath. "I think I owe you an apology."

Chloe blinked rapidly. Obviously, the words were the last ones she expected from the other woman's mouth. "Oh."

"I shouldn't have shouted at you, or made you feel bad. It's just, well, I guess I'm committed now. I'm jealous of you," Megan admitted, stumbling over the words, forcing them out.

Chloe's mouth dropped open. "Say what? You're jealous of me?"

"Yeah." Megan began to feel a little silly at having felt that way at all.

"But you're you!" Chloe said in disbelief.

"What?" Megan was uncertain of what, exactly, the girl was getting at.

"You're amazing. Like, my gosh, I wish I was like you."

Megan looked at Chloe like she'd lost her mind. "Excuse me?"

"Um, I try to be like you. You're smart and, what I like best, you really don't care what people think. You live your life how you want to. I think that's awesome."

Megan puffed out a breath of air. "I wouldn't exactly say that, but I guess the main thing is, are we good?"

Chloe threw her arms around Megan. "We're more than good."

"Okay then, we'd better get back the party. We wouldn't want Travis to be lonely." Megan winked at Chloe.

The girl blushed. "Is it that obvious?"

"Yeah."

"Do you think he knows?" Chloe looked horrified at the thought.

"I'm pretty sure he doesn't have a clue. Most of the time, men don't until it smacks them in the face."

"Is that what Carlos is like?"

"Excuse me?" Megan looked sharply at Chloe.

Surprisingly, her friend held her gaze, unflinching. "He doesn't know you like him, right?"

"Who says I do?" Megan denied, trying to appear nonchalant.

Chloe giggled mischievously and merrily headed outside. "Whatever you say."

CHAPTER 7

The sharp sting of a horse-fly on her arm prompted Megan to slap out in retaliation. She felt a sense of kinship to the band of broodmares grazing before her, periodically swishing their tails through the air at the pests. Megan squinted in concentration as she peered at one of the horses. Something wasn't right. She leaned in, trying to get a closer look, scowling in frustration when she couldn't quite put her finger on what it was exactly. Listening to the concerned feeling that crept over her, she reached to unbuckle the spare halter from the gate. Whistling softly, she approached the group and secured the chestnut mare in question.

Alarm spiked through Megan when she noticed that the mare had already developed an udder and was dripping milk. "No, no, no. This is way too early." She rapidly went through her options and, deciding she would rather look foolish for overreacting, she came to her decision. Leading the animal through the gate, she made her way toward the barn. Spying Deb, she waved to get her attention. "Deb, I'm taking Rosie across to the vet barn now. Call Carlos and tell him to expect me."

Deb nodded her understanding, homing in on the urgency vibrating off her friend. "What do you think is wrong?"

"She's getting ready to foal way too bloody early. I need him to check her over and find out why."

"I'll let him know." Deb watched the departing mare with concern-filled eyes. "You hold onto that bloody foal, Rosie, do you hear me?"

CARLOS WAS WAITING, the crush prepared with his equipment at the ready, when Megan arrived, Rosie in tow. "Let's get her in here and I'll check her over. What were the symptoms that concerned you?" he asked professionally.

"Her udder is developing too early and it's already leaking milk. I think she has some discharge from her vulva as well." Megan stood quietly, her palms sweaty as she stroked Rosie, praying that she was wrong. She kept a close eye on Carlos as he made his preliminary examination, no hint of his diagnosis in his expression as he worked.

Completing his assessment, he returned to stand with Megan at the mare's head. "You were right to bring her. I want to do both an internal and external ultrasound." His cool, professional tone was at odds with his grim expression.

"Do you think it's placentitis?" Megan probed, her eyes shadowed with worry. She knew what was at stake if it was.

Carlos wheeled the machine closer to the equine crush, pressing a button. The screen began to glow. "I'll know more after the scans," he replied, looking grimly at her. "But I think you might be right." Applying lubricant to the wand, he patted Rosie on the rump. "Someone once told me that I need to take my time with these sorts of things, but you'll forgive me, darlin', if I take things a bit fast. We need to find out what's going on with your baby."

Megan smiled at Carlos's conversation with the expectant mare. Given her stress levels, it surprised her that he could have that effect on her. "I think your bedside manner is improving."

The look he leveled at her was pure male promise. "I can guarantee I've never had any complaints about my bedside manner, in or anywhere near a bed."

"Focus," Megan said, laughing despite her concern for Rosie and her foal.

"I am. Okay, that isn't what I wanted to see. The uterus and placenta have a pronounced increase in thickness. She definitely has an infection there and you were on the money —she has placentitis. I'm going to do the external abdominal scan now and assess the fetal wellbeing." He moved around to Rosie's side. "The heartbeat seems good and the foal is a good size." Carlos gave the mare a soothing stroke before stepping back and beginning to pack up his equipment.

"What antibiotics will you use? Will you be testing her mammary electrolytes to see how close she is to foaling?"

Carlos gave her an admiring look. "Except for my boyish charm, I'm not sure you need me to treat her. I think you would be just fine on your own." Warmth flooded through Megan's body at his approval.

"I've had to help with a few cases like this back home at the thoroughbred stud I used to work at," she explained.

"First, I need to do a swab of her cervix to determine what the causative agent is so I can prescribe the most suitable antibiotic. And yes, I'll run a test to see how close she is to foaling."

Megan nodded, her mind already racing ahead to the care

Rosie would need. "She's going to need close monitoring, isn't she?"

"Which, lucky for her, I have no other patients, making her my sole priority." Carlos sent Megan a reassuring smile. "I'll make sure she's well looked after, but if you like or, should I say, if you don't trust me, you're more than welcome to assist me in her care."

Embarrassed, Megan returned his smile, conscious he now stood at Rosie's head with her. "I didn't mean to imply that you wouldn't do a bloody good job, it's just that I feel responsible for her."

"Then we look forward to seeing you when you check up on us." He gave the horse a rub on her nose. "Don't we, Rosie?"

Deciding that having Carlos standing in such close proximity was having an entirely unacceptable impact on her heartbeat, she stepped back. "I guess I'd better leave the two of you to get better acquainted."

Carlos unlatched the crush and backed Rosie out. "Once I've given her the first course of antibiotics and have her settled, I was going to make myself a cup of coffee. There's even some doughnuts that aren't too stale if you'd like to join me?" he asked casually, leading the chestnut horse to a stall.

Her dang heart, having only just settled down, started pounding again. "Um, maybe not today, I've got a lot left to do. I kinda dropped everything to get Rosie over here and the others will want to know what's happened, so..." Megan rambled, her eyes flitting everywhere, except to meet Carlos's.

He gave a little laugh as if he could see through her excuses. "Well, then, I'll take a raincheck. Next time, I'll try to have something a bit more tempting." Seriously, the man could have offered stale bread and it would have still been tempting. "Oh, Megan?"

"Yeah."

"I plan on collecting on it, too."

THE SCRATCH of rake tines against the concrete floor drew Megan's attention as she entered the vet barn. She'd flown through her responsibilities back at the stud in record time. The girls, concerned for the mare's wellbeing, had peppered her with questions, slowing her down. Anxious to return and see how the sick mare had responded to beginning treatment, she had finally managed to suitably allay their fears and escape. If she was honest with herself, seeing Carlos again had been a motivating factor in her haste.

Following the noise, she was surprised to find the handsome vet cleaning out Rosie's stall, the chestnut mare standing in the way as she tried to solicit more attention from him. Megan laughed at the scene.

"I didn't know they taught stall cleaning at vet school," she teased. "Or how to deal with flirtatious mares."

"I am more than a pretty face." He gave her his best blue steel look. "Which, you have to agree, is one of my best features."

"If you say so." Megan spluttered with laughter.

"Anyway, I'll have you know, I passed Stableboy 101 with flying colors." He gave the straw one last pass-through with the rake and headed to the stall door, giving Rosie a pat on the way through. Megan swore the mare made winsome eyes at him.

Holding the door open for him, Megan blocked the mare's attempt to follow the man out. "I see you have a new friend."

"What can I say? All females love me." Carlos was the

picture of modesty as he headed to the manure pile to empty his bucket.

"Sure, whatever you say." Megan's voice dripped with sarcasm. "How's she responding?"

"It's still too early to say. She hasn't gotten worse, but time will tell if we can stop the infection in time. Now, since I have an hour or so till I next have to check on my number one patient, would you like to have dinner with me?" He glanced down at his dirty clothes. "Well, after I clean up a bit. If it helps, I cooked it myself."

Megan thought he looked just fine as he was, but she'd rather bite off her own tongue than admit that to him. "You cooked? I don't know if that's a good thing or not."

He shot her a lingering look, his dark eyes gleaming with a wicked challenge. "I'm good at being good, and good at being bad. It just depends what the lady wants."

Megan's mouth went dry at his words. Finally, finding her voice, she put her hands tartly on her hips. "I believe we were talking about cooking."

Those mercurial dark eyes of his turned amused. "Well, as it happens, I'm excellent at cooking. I should be. I learned from the best—my mae."

"Why do I feel like I'm going to regret this?" Megan wondered aloud.

"If that's you graciously accepting my kind offer of sustenance, then I promise you won't regret a thing."

THE GRAVY WAS STUPENDOUSLY rich and complex, the seasoning dancing across the palate. Megan raised her eyebrows in appreciation as she took another bite of the stew. "I'm impressed," she admitted.

"I knew you would be. I'm an impressive kind of guy."

Carlos humbly shrugged. "I'm not sure why you haven't noticed that before. Maybe you need to pay closer attention."

Megan gave him a long-suffering glare—one she usually reserved for Deb—mainly to hide the fact that she had been paying him a lot of attention. "And there's that modesty again."

"Well, when you have the mother I have, it would've been criminal for me not to be a superior cook."

"That's true. The only thing my mom ever fed us was bloody meat pies from the freezer." Even now, she couldn't stand the smell of a pie being heated up in the oven.

"I don't think I've ever had an Aussie meat pie before."

"Do yourself a favor, if you're going to have one for the first time, get Frankie to make you some. Not the horrible frozen kind that I grew up on."

"You have a good instinct with sick animals," Carlos said, leaving Megan disorientated at the sudden change in topic.

"Thanks, I guess," she replied around another mouthful of stew.

"Is this what you've always dreamed of doing?"

"Having dinner with a hot guy? Sure." Megan silently cursed her loose tongue for betraying her.

His answering smile was smugly pleased, the dimples in full effect. "So, you do find me good looking. I knew it was only a matter of time before you could no longer resist my charms. But what I meant was what you're doing now, working with horses. Is that all you ever wanted to do? If you don't mind me saying, you don't seem to have the same intensity to your passion working with them as the others. Me, I always knew that I wanted to help. But it took me a little while to figure out that I wanted to help animals more than humans."

Megan hovered indecisively over her words, unsure how much to share. "Well, when I was younger, I wanted to be a vet like you." She smiled sadly. "But my upbringing was"—she hesitated—"tough. I was out of home as soon as I could and, for me, that meant taking a job at the local thoroughbred stud because it included accommodation. I met my first boyfriend there." It surprised her that, after all this time, just thinking about him could still fill her with the worthlessness his cold words had left her with.

Carlos topped up her wineglass, his face sympathetic. "I take it from your expression that it didn't end well?"

"You could say that," Megan said bitterly, taking a sip of her refreshed wine. "He was the son of the stud manager and I'm sure you would know from your time in Kentucky that thoroughbred studs attract lots of young, good-looking girls. Eventually, he found one who was better looking and had a better family than mine. He made sure I knew exactly why he was replacing me, too." There it was. The frigid feeling of humiliation sliding alongside the bitter worthlessness.

Carlos reached his hand out, capturing hers. The warmth of his touch chased away the cold, her dark emotions fleeing before it. "Then he was an idiot."

CHAPTER 8

*H*er hand, sweaty on the doorknob, hesitated. Inside, Megan could hear the clink of a spoon against a mug, a chair scraping against the timber floorboards. It had been pure bliss to wake up that morning, the sun still tucked in bed and everyone else in the bunkhouse sound asleep. She had prudently exited the dwelling before any of her friends could grill her over her previous night's activities. Blowing out her cheeks in defeat, she bowed before the inevitable and entered the room.

"Looking a bit hot and bothered there," Deb greeted her. "But I guess I would be too if I had just had an intimate dinner with Carlos Dreamypants."

"Carlos Dreamypants." Chloe giggled. "That's actually pretty funny."

Mitch secured Grace in her highchair. "She just came back from a run. Of course she's bloody red faced and sweaty." Megan threw him a grateful look as he settled down to supervise his daughter's breakfast. "But she could just be blowing some steam off after her hot date." Megan's look rapidly darkened at his betrayal.

"I guess I should be thankful that Gabi and Frankie aren't here yet," Megan muttered, grabbing a piece of toast off Deb's plate.

"Oy, you!" Deb grabbed for the heisted bread.

"Serves you right," Megan countered, dodging out of reach. "Just so everyone is clear, what happened last night is—"

Mitch covered Grace's ears, the little girl protesting and trying to pull his hands off. "Gracie, love, you're too young to hear what Megan's about to say."

Chloe giggled, the mirthful sound ceasing at Megan's threatening glare.

"To be clear, he shared his dinner with me. Nothing. Else."

"I'm disappointed," Deb said, shaking her head. "Carlos Dreamypants all to yourself and you wasted a perfectly good opportunity to, well, get into his dreamy pants."

Chloe spluttered on her coffee and Mitch helpfully pounded her on the back. Grace took the opportunity to throw her scrambled eggs on the floor.

Megan turned her back on the chaos, electing to head to the shower. "I'm not even going to dignify that with a bloody answer. But I'll say this, if I did, you'd be the last to know." She closed the bathroom door on their shocked faces.

MEGAN KEPT GLANCING down at her watch, seriously tempted to tap it on the table to make sure it was still working. She had flown through her morning work with the aim of visiting Rosie before she was needed back for afternoon tasks, and then it had happened—Gabi had swanned in with her laptop and notes and reminded everyone that they had a meeting.

"Bloody meetings," Megan muttered under her breath.

Gabi raised her eyebrows. "I'm sorry, I didn't quite catch that."

Megan shook her head. "Just thinking aloud, Gabi. Sorry, I didn't mean to interrupt." She picked up her pen and started doodling. "I wouldn't want to make this bloody meeting go any longer than it has to." This time, she murmured it much quieter.

Chloe giggled, drawing Gabi's suspicious gaze. "Anyway, as I was saying, the clinic was a huge success. We already have a waiting list for the next one that is, at this stage, humungous."

"We might need a few more buckets located discreetly around the arena," Deb said over the top of Frankie's dismayed groan at the news.

"I don't know if my nerves will hold out with a bigger crowd," Frankie wailed.

"We'll keep the same numbers as last time. I think that size worked well. It gives it a more intimate feeling," reassured Gabi. "But with standing waiting lists, we can start advertising it as a premium event."

"And charge accordingly," noted Deb.

"Well yes, but no." Gabi giggled at her own contradiction. "I think we charged fairly for the last one and just because we could ask for more money, I don't think we need to." She pursed her lips. "Long term, if we keep this up, we'll need to put some thought into upgrading facilities. This place was never designed to be a training and clinic hosting ranch."

"I also got feedback on the day that people really felt like they benefited from the assistance Chloe gave them," Frankie said, causing the young woman to blush.

"It was nothing, just doing my job."

Gabi nodded in agreement with Frankie. "I received the same feedback—even a couple of emails from parents saying how much their kids liked Chloe and enjoyed learning from her."

"Sounds like you're a bit of a natural," Megan complimented the embarrassed young woman.

"Thanks guys, I really enjoyed it."

"How have the renovations been going at your place?" Frankie looked over her coffee cup to Gabi.

"Pretty good actually. Did you know that Bryce is a silent partner in Jade's interior design firm?" Gabi gave an impressed shake of her head.

"Doesn't surprise me. That man has a lot of fingers in pies," Megan said, glancing at her watch again.

A knock on the door interrupted the conversation. "Come in," Deb hollered.

Carlos popped his head through the door he partially opened. "Can I borrow Megan for a second?"

Four pairs of wildly curious eyes focused on Megan. "Um, sure," she said, rising from her seat. "Not a word from any of you," she muttered as she walked past her friends. Once she had safely made it outside, she looked at the vet in alarm, suddenly considering that he might be there because of an issue with his patient. "Is everything okay? With Rosie?"

"Oh, yeah, everything's fine with the mare." He looked down at his hands. For the first time, Megan noticed that they held a large envelope. "The other day, when we had dinner, you mentioned you wanted to be a vet."

Megan's forehead wrinkled in confusion. "Yeah, that was a bloody long time ago."

His dark eyes locked with her green ones. "I think you should pursue it. You have really good instincts and, honestly, that's the hardest bit to learn."

Megan was taken aback at his words. She stood stock still, made silent by the unfamiliar feeling of respect and encouragement Carlos projected at her. "Um, well, thanks. I guess I might look into it a bit when I get a chance."

"I already know the local college has a good course. A friend of mine is a professor there." He held the envelope out to her. "I took the liberty of getting an application for you. I wasn't trying to intrude." He paused, looking down at their two hands, linked by the paper between them. He swallowed before returning his intense gaze back to hers. "I think you should do this, for you."

Somehow, it felt like he was trying to say more. But what confused Megan the most was why it seemed so important to him. She nodded. "I need to think about it."

Carlos finally let go of the envelope, leaving Megan feeling like she had been cut adrift. "Please do. And I mean that. Really think about it, okay?" Seemingly satisfied by what he saw in her face, he left her to contemplate his words.

Megan was, quite simply, at a loss as to why he had gone to so much effort for her. Thinking about the intense look in those gorgeous eyes of his and the firm way he had insisted she think about it did funny things to her belly. She knew that, as soon as she stepped back through that door, her friends would have a field day teasing her. *Why me?* She briefly contemplated hiding for the rest of the day before discarding the idea. Knowing her friends, they would hunt her down until they got their answers. Apparently, it was true. There really was no rest or, in this case, peace for the wicked. Sighing in defeat, she headed back inside.

CHAPTER 9

There comes a point with exhaustion, where, even though the body is fatigued, the mind is somehow set free, drifting unhindered from its earthly binding. The days had been hectic. Frankie was back on the road again, and Gabi flitted between business meetings, renovations, rodeos and the ranch. Honestly, Megan didn't mind much that Gabi wasn't there as often as usual. It gave her a chance to catch up on work without the constant meetings.

And then, there was Carlos. He was always there either giving her updates on Rosie—who was responding well to the antibiotics but was still deemed a high-risk pregnancy—or in her thoughts. Such was the case this evening. After Chloe had said goodnight and retired to her room, Megan had found herself thinking about him as she stared down at the application paperwork. She startled when Deb came into the room.

"I was just coming out to turn the lights off," Deb said quietly. "I thought everyone had gone to bed. Mitch is already snoring. I don't know how much sugar Grace had today but, my gosh, it was a bloody battle to get her settled. She just wanted to keep playing."

Megan scooted over to make room for Deb on the sofa. "I want to go to bed, but I don't have enough energy to even stand up."

Her friend laughed. "Dang, I know that feeling well." Deb looked curiously down at the paper in Megan's hand. "Does the reason you're still awake have anything to do with what's in your hand?"

Megan tilted her head from side to side, considering whether or not to share. The small flicker of confidence that Carlos had lit within her was a fragile thing. One indelicate huff would be enough to extinguish it. Deciding she would, at some point, have to tell her friends, she still paused before sheer force of will brought the words to her mouth.

"This is the paperwork to apply to college to become a vet." She hesitantly looked up at Deb to gauge her reaction.

"That's awesome. You'd make a bloody tiptop vet."

Megan blinked. Her friend's unreserved approval meant more to her than she wanted to admit. "Thanks. I'm not sure if I am going to fill it in or not yet."

"Why?"

Her fingers played with the corner of the paper in her hand. "I don't know. It's just a big thing to do, you know?"

Deb nodded. "It bloody is. But I remember, when we were teenagers, that's all you used to want to be. You were always trying to help wounded and sick animals, patching them up. I remember you trying to make little splints and everything."

Megan tugged on her bottom lip. "I mean, I might not get in and, if I did, it's going to take up an awful lot of time. It's pretty busy around here."

"Let me ask you this. What made you get the application now?"

She coughed uncomfortably. "Um, I didn't."

Deb laughed in sudden understanding. "Is this what Carlos wanted to see you about the other day?"

"Yeah."

"I'm impressed that it's taken you this long to finally spill. We put you under serious pressure and you didn't even come close to cracking." Deb rubbed her ear absentmindedly. "I think Carlos is a really good vet and a pretty smart guy. If he thinks you have what it takes, then you should listen." Deb's face grew serious. "Megan, I know things weren't great when you were growing up. Everything you have, you've earned the hard way. And none of the others are here right now, but I know they'd say the same thing. If you want to do this, we'll find a way to make it work. It's okay to chase your dreams, too."

Megan swallowed, blinking away the sudden moisture in her eyes. "Thanks, Deb. I didn't know I needed to hear that until you said it."

"Anytime. Now, I'm going to try and get some sleep over the rattling of Mitch's snoring." Deb hesitated on the cusp of leaving the room. "Megan, I know you and I haven't always seen eye to eye, but you are still one of my best friends. I will never forget what you did for me when, well, Tucker. We're family, and I will support you no matter what you decide." Her voice suddenly shaky, she quietly left the room.

Megan sat on that old sofa for a long time letting her friend's words wash some of life's hurt away.

～

"Do you have plans tonight?"

Megan, who had been struggling to get a comb through Rosie's tail, must have tugged a little too hard in surprise, causing the mare to swish her tail in protest. The sting of the hair whipping her in the face prompted Megan to cry out.

Holding a hand to her sore cheek, she peered at Carlos. "I beg your pardon?"

There was a hint of dimples that made Megan suspect he was trying hard not to laugh at her misfortune. "Are you free tonight?"

"I'll have you know, I've very expensive most nights," she tartly replied, grabbing a body brush and setting to work on the pregnant mare's coat. "But let me check my schedule." She made a pretense of perusing a make-believe diary. "Hmm, looks like I'll be doing the same thing I do every night when I finish work. A big fat nothing."

"Good. I'll pick you up around eight then."

"Why?" Megan asked. Was he asking her out?

Carlos raised an eyebrow at the ungracious tone. "Firstly, I would actually like to take you out to dinner. I like you, and it shouldn't be too much of a surprise that I'd like to take you out on a date. Secondly, a little birdie at the college told me you had submitted your paperwork and I thought that was worth a celebration." He sent her a challenging look. "Unless you have any objections to being seen in public with me?"

Megan appraised his tall, broad-shouldered frame, appreciating the way he filled out the denim of his jeans. Doubt squirreled into her mind, reminding her of her shorter, curvy stature. Her apprehension must have shown on her face.

"Don't you dare chicken out of my invitation."

Megan raised her chin defiantly. "I wasn't going to."

"Good. I'll see you at eight then."

WOODEN STOOLS BUTTED up against the brass footrail at the high counter. Patrons laughed and chatted over their drinks, their reflections dancing in the mirror behind the bar. The bar was dim and loud, lit up by large neon signs, the walls lined with memorabilia. Megan trailed behind Carlos, holding his hand tightly as they weaved their way through the crowd to order their drinks. She glanced curiously around, watching the dancers stomp their boots and clap to the music. There was a sense of irresistible mystique to the night. She wondered how it would evolve.

Megan returned her attention to Carlos as he handed her a beer, the glass clinking as they touched their bottles together. As she took a sip, he leaned in closer, his breath moist on her ear. "You look very beautiful tonight."

She looked down at her dress. Megan had actually put a bit of effort into getting her outfit together, even enlisting the aid of Chloe and Deb. She laughed lightly. "This old thing? I guess it's a bit different to what I usually wear."

"You'll get no complaints from me. I like you in whatever you have on—or nothing, as the case may be." Pure masculine approval shone from his eyes, leaving her in no doubt what he would prefer her to be wearing.

She almost spluttered out her beer at his words and direct look. "Wow. You buy a girl one bloody drink and, next thing, you're trying to get her out of her clothes."

He winked at her. "Always. But first, let's dance." He grabbed her hand and led her to the dance floor. To her surprise, the music had changed to a slow number, the couples now together in tight embraces, their bodies intertwined as they swayed in the dim light. Carlos pulled her into his arms, his hand warm on the small of her back. As they swayed gently together, Megan marveled at how strong and, at the same time, vulnerable he made her feel. It was no longer possible for her to pretend that he was just some hot guy. She wasn't sure how, but she had fallen for Carlos Cabrera.

Somehow sensing the softening in her demeanor, Carlos

looked down at her intently, his gaze drawn to her ripe mouth. A fluttering of desire rippled through her. The excitement of kissing Carlos, the deliciousness of what it would be like, set her heart racing. His lips were commanding against hers. The man was clearly experienced, and it felt good and terrifyingly right. *Perhaps*, Megan thought to herself. *This is a gift, the chance to start a grown-up relationship with someone who gets me, and I get them.*

As Carlos pulled back from the kiss, he stared at her in wonderment. "My beautiful little Megan. I don't know what I did to deserve finding you, but I thank God I did."

CHAPTER 10

Megan stared, entranced by the sunlight filtering in through the kitchen window. The light glistened and sparkled joyously. The coffee tickled her nostrils, rich and complex in odor. She felt as if she was viewing the world through a new lens—richer and serene. An exquisite sensation of all tension left her body, causing her to smile.

"Okay, who are you and what have you done with Megan?" Deb tapped her lightly on the head. "I know you're in there. Blink twice if you need help."

"It's too nice a day to even let your bad jokes ruin it," Megan said, poking her tongue out. She wrapped her arms around her body as if to hold the euphoric feeling close. "You know what? It's too bloody nice a day to stay inside. I think I'll take my coffee and enjoy it outside." Decisively, she opened the door and stopped dead. On the doorstep was a plush white teddy bear, his little nose shaped like a love heart and, in his paw, he held a single white rose. Megan stooped and picked him up. A note fluttered to the ground. Retrieving it, she began to read.

. . .

Sometimes the most beautiful of flowers requires the patience to get past the thorns and bramble. But that only makes them more precious.

Warmth infused Megan's body, the tingling surge beginning in her chest and spreading outward.

"From Mr Dreamypants?" Deb asked, peering at the gift.

"Yes." Megan held the dear bear close, her smile beaming.

"I think that's so sweet," Chloe breathed. "It's like a romantic fairy tale."

Grace, spotting the bear, began to clamor for it. Megan knelt and swept the little girl into a hug, allowing her to hold the gift. Feeling her mind empty of all cares, she let out an unrestrained laugh, luxuriating in the total sense of freedom.

"Now you're really starting to freak me out," Deb declared, washing her dishes in the sink. "It's just not natural for you to be this happy."

Megan smiled sweetly at her. "Better bloody get used to it. I think I'm going to feel this way a lot from now on."

Joao accepted the beer from Carlos. "How do you like being back home?"

Carlos sat down on the sofa, resting his sock clad feet on the table in front of him. "I think it was just what the doctor ordered."

"The human doctor or the animal doctor?" Joao queried slyly. "I take it you have mended your broken heart?"

"Not to take anything away from Evangeline—I really did care about her. But man, I don't think anyone has made me feel the way Megan does." He sipped his beer, his heart racing at the mere thought of the little Australian firecracker. "She's so hard on the outside, but she has her reasons and, honestly, I respect her an awful lot more knowing what she went through. She's tough, but, phew." He blew out a breath. "Inside that shell, she's one heck of a woman. A woman I want to protect and, at the same time, let her be her. It's crazy."

Joao smirked. "The mighty Carlos Cabrera, lover of women, appreciator of the fine female form. Sounds like you have it bad for Megan."

"I do." He grinned at his friend. "I really do." He drained his beer and held up the empty bottle. "Another?"

"Well, we are celebrating after all."

Carlos grinned. "And my darling sister is on the road with Frankie?" he teased.

Joao ruefully returned his smile. "That too."

A PLEASANT GLOW that can only reliably be achieved by indulging in the company of good friends or, in this case, best friend and a steady supply of beer wrapped its welcoming arms around Carlos as he bid Joao a wobbly goodnight. Staggering back to the sofa, he sat back down, smiling drunkenly in his contentment at the situation. A knock at the door made him rise, albeit unsteadily, to his feet and, like a sailor on a storm-tossed ship, he carefully traversed the length of his living room to the door.

"Did you forget your way home, Joao?" he slurred, leaning on the door for support.

"I know how to get home and I have no idea who this Joao is," a crisply unamused voice answered.

The voice was strangely familiar. The rounded shape was

not. Blinking his bleary eyes to clear the alcohol-induced fog from them, he peered owlishly at the figure before him. His eyes flew wide in sudden realization of who it was. Evangeline. A very pregnant Evangeline—his ex-girlfriend.

"COFFEE. I NEED COFFEE." Hand trembling, he poured the granules into the percolator, brown grounds spilling onto the bench.

"Well, I must say, this wasn't the state that I was expecting to find you in." She sniffed haughtily in disapproval at his drunken manner.

"I could say the same for you," he quickly rebutted, mentally high fiving himself on the sharp retort. Deciding the coffee had brewed long enough, he filled his cup, choking on the lukewarm bitterness. "Why are you here, Evangeline?"

She looked down at her extended belly. "I would think that was fairly obvious."

"You're saying it's mine?" Carlos wasn't sure what was sobering him up faster—the tepid brew or her words.

She glared at him belligerently. "Of course it's yours. Who else would it be?"

"Well, I don't know, you can't blame me for asking. I thought we had a good thing going and then you broke up with me and I don't hear a thing from you till you show up at my door with a baby in your belly." Seeing that she was on the verge of tears, his expression softened. He gently guided her to the sofa. "Why did it take you so long to tell me? Why would you not let me know I was going to be a father?"

She sniffled miserably. "I was scared. I didn't know after how I treated you when we broke up if you would want anything to do with me." She cradled her stomach possessively. "With us," she corrected herself, sobbing. "Our baby needs his daddy and so do I."

He pulled the crying mother-to-be into his arms. His entire world rocked on its axis. Still partially held in alcohol's sway, Carlos wondered how on earth he was going to break the news to Megan.

CHAPTER 11

The pounding of his head was the only thing that kept Carlos from thinking last night hadn't been a bad dream. He squinted his eyes against the bright morning light, cursing that drunk Carlos hadn't closed the curtain better the previous evening. Coffee granules crunched underfoot as he grabbed a dirty mug from the sink and filled it, not caring about anything except making the pounding stop. He buried his head in his hands, no longer sure what hurt more—his head or his heart. One thing he knew for sure, one would feel better by the end of the day. The other, well, it might never feel whole again.

"If I didn't know better, I would think you were avoiding me."

Megan cringed at how clingy she sounded. Sure, she hadn't seen him around for a few days and he hadn't returned her messages, but the man probably didn't want to rush what they had. Nice and slow. That's what they needed to do. She smiled, trying to take the edge off her previous words. The smile slid off her face when she registered the expression on Carlos's face. He looked like he had just swallowed a fly fresh from the manure pile.

"Are you okay?"

He smiled, one that she noted didn't reach his eyes, his dimples hiding. "I have something I need to tell you and I've been trying to find the best way. But I don't think there is."

A cold wash of apprehension cascaded over Megan, settling in a cold lump in her chest. "This sounds serious," she said, striving to maintain a lighthearted mood, despite the tightness banding around her ribs. "Should I sit down?"

Carlos averted his eyes. "Maybe you should."

The cold lump turned to lead, settling heavy around her heart. "Surely it can't be that bloody serious?"

His expression became haunted. "I don't know where to begin."

"Try the beginning." Megan tried to keep the fear from her voice, the tension thick between them.

"My ex-girlfriend turned up the other night and—"

Megan held a shaky hand to her brow, "You don't need to finish that." She shook her head bitterly. "I already know how that particular story ends."

"No, you don't."

"No? It's not the one where you break up with me for your beautiful, rich ex-girlfriend?" Seeing no denial on his face, she agitatedly rubbed at her face. "I am such an idiot. This was never going to work. I should've known I wasn't good enough." Her voice was sharp, devastation cutting through her.

"Have you ever thought you were enough?" Carlos angrily stalked closer, pulling her hand away from her face. "That you don't need to come from money or a rich family? That I don't care, that all I want is you?" His anguished eyes snared hers, holding her captive.

"Well, apparently I'm not enough if we're having this bloody conversation." Megan took a step back, needing space between them.

Carlos, not having any of it, closed it again. "Megan, she's pregnant. Even though it's killing me to walk away from this thing between us—and I know you feel it too—I have to do the honorable thing." His voice shook with the rawness of his emotion. "Megan, you have no idea how hard I fell for you."

Megan exhaled sadly, surprised she could even draw breath around the vice-like grip despair had on her heart. "It doesn't really bloody matter anymore, does it?"

He grabbed her arm. "It matters a lot. You're special, Megan."

Not special enough, the insidious voice whispered, awakening from its hibernation. *Never special enough to anyone.*

THE TEDDY BEAR had long ago turned into a sodden mess. Megan lay spent on her side, wrapped around the toy. The creak of her door was followed by quick, short steps before her bed springs creaked under the additional weight that climbed aboard. A small, warm body draped itself over her, smelling of sunshine and cookies.

"You give the best hugs, Gracie." Megan sniffled.

"That's why we sent her in first." Deb entered the room.

"My plan was to keep slipping chocolate under the door until you felt better." Chloe sat on the bed beside Deb.

"I said her plan was clearly not going to work," Gabi asserted, holding up some beers.

"We told her a girl needs something stronger in a time

like this," Frankie agreed, holding up more beers. "If this doesn't hit the spot, we can always do shots."

"I appreciate what you guys are doing, I really do. But I need to deal with this by myself." Megan was mortified at the trembling in her voice. Mortified, and so tired of having to push all hints of vulnerability down, to hide it away. *No one likes a crybaby.* The voice made its presence known. *Better they think you're a cow than weak.*

The girls looked at each other uncertainly. "Um, well, I mean, we don't have to drink. We can do whatever you want," Frankie said.

"I really just want to be alone." Megan stared into the damp fur of her bear.

"Come on, Gracie. Auntie Megan needs to be alone. Your hugs have made her feel a lot better." The little girl gave Megan a sloppy kiss and climbed down at her mother's urging.

"Wove you, Mwegan."

"Love you too, Gracie." There was something about the innocent, purity of the little girl's declaration of love that made Megan want to weep.

Frankie ushered the other girls out before hesitating on the threshold. "Megan, if you change your mind, well, we all love you." She silently slipped out, closing the door behind her.

Megan buried her face in the soggy fur and silently cried, trying to purge the pain of her broken heart.

SRA ANA HAD, even by her usual standards, outdone herself. Delicious and fragrant aromas wafted from the dishes set in the center of the table. "Please, fill your plate Evangeline. I can give you the recipes later if you wish. They are some of Carlos's favorites."

Evangeline delicately held a napkin to her mouth. "They smell … quite strong. Our family cook is French, and I am sure Carlos enjoys them just as much as he did when we visited my family in The Hamptons." She turned to Carlos and held out her glass. "Can you please get me some more water?"

Carlos couldn't take Gabi staring stonily across the table at him any longer, grateful for a reason to escape her relentless judgement, he excused himself from the table. "Our mae's cooking is legendary. I think I'll help Carlos with that water." Gabi said. Carlos caught Joao sending Gabi a warning look, one she chose to ignore. Knowing she would be hot on his heels as he heard her excuse herself from the table, he increased his pace.

"I hope you know what you're doing," she whispered furiously once she'd entered the kitchen.

"Honestly, I haven't got a clue." Carlos rubbed his tired eyes. "I can tell you that this sure as heck isn't what I imagined I would be doing a week ago, or who I'd be doing it with."

"Well, I left Megan crying herself dry over that stupid teddy bear you gave her. I'm so mad at you right now I could spit."

Carlos hung his head. Everything about him screamed out his anguish. "I never expected to feel how I did about Megan, but it was real." He didn't want to see the flash of sympathy on Gabi's face, it was hard enough admitting how hard he had fallen for her friend.

"I might not know her as well as the other girls do, but I've never seen her so … exposed? It was like something happened when you guys got to know each other and she didn't need to hide the real her anymore. There was a happiness to her."

"It's one of the hardest things I've ever had to do. Walking away from that, from her," Carlos admitted. "But Mae and Papai raised us to do the right thing and the right thing to do here is to not abandon the mother of my child. I have to think about my baby. No matter how much my heart yearns for someone else."

Carlos was so lost in his own pain that he was caught by surprise when Gabi pulled him into a fierce hug. Outside, unaware to both of them, the subject of their conversation lingered, listening to every word they had uttered. Evangeline, having excused herself to use the bathroom had found the opportunity to eavesdrop too tempting. Hearing them begin to return, she quickly hurried out of sight.

CHAPTER 12

Everyone must think I'm so stupid for thinking I could keep someone like Carlos interested. Megan looked across the barn aisle to where Gabi was in a discussion with the cause of her heartbreak, Gabi suddenly chuckling as her brother grinned at her sheepishly. The two of them were probably laughing at her and her naivety right now. *Well, that stops right this minute.*

It had felt like a kick in the guts when she found out about the Cabrera family dinner that Evangeline had attended. Her treacherous heart had wallowed in misery, wondering if she would have been welcomed so enthusiastically. The inner voice that had been dormant sprung to life, whispering bile into her mind, assuring her she would never have been treated how the perfect Evangeline was being treated. No matter how hard she tried, now that it was released from its box, nothing could silence the self-loathing thoughts.

I'm never going to let someone make me that vulnerable again, she promised herself. After all, if her upbringing had taught her anything, it was to look after yourself and never show weakness. She returned to preparing the stall for foaling down, stabbing viciously at the straw with her pitchfork. If Megan had but looked up, she would have seen Carlos hesitate as he walked away from his sister, his head pulled against his will in her direction as longing for her flowed from his eyes. But alas, she did not.

"You know, I don't even like her that much." Megan's head jerked up in surprise to find Gabi leaning over the stable door.

"I don't know who you're talking about." Megan returned to stabbing at the offending straw.

Gabi's answering laugh stiffened Megan's spine. "Okay, Megan, but all of this"—she did a circling gesture taking in Megan's posture and attitude—"tells me that you know exactly who I'm talking about."

"Fine." Megan stopped her attack on the straw and folded her arms across her chest, glaring at the other girl. "But you could've fooled me. Seems like you're all one big happy family with your dinners and everything."

Gabi sighed. "I'm not really sure my parents like her either. And please don't take this the wrong way, but they aren't being disloyal to you by inviting her to dinner. They still love you, and if things had been different … well…" Her voice trailed off.

"But they're not."

"No, and we can't change that. All we can do is try and make the best of it." Gabi's eyes searched Megan's face to see if any of her words were making an impact on her friend. "Papai and Mae are probably two of the most generous, caring people you will meet, and Evangeline is carrying their unborn grandbaby. No matter how difficult she makes it for them, they'll always try and make her feel welcome."

"I know how much this baby must mean to your parents. It's just, well…"

"Sucky?"

"Yeah. Really sucky." Megan returned to her task, calmer this time. The edge of her anger had retreated, leaving only a deep sorrow.

"Megan, I know Carlos wished it was different, too." Gabi's voice was soft as she offered her commiseration.

"Yeah, well, wishes were horses and all that." She turned her back so that Gabi could not see the silent tear that trekked down her face. Megan pushed the hurt and pain tightly inside, ignorant to the fact that wounds to the heart must see the light of day, otherwise, if left to fester, they could turn the soul septic.

Sra Ana offered the plate of cookies to her guest, watching as Evangeline crinkled her nose in disgust. "I don't eat anything that doesn't have at least three superfoods in it," came the rebuttal, said in a superior tone that matched her attitude.

Sra Ana took two just to be perverse and lowered the plate to the table. "How have you been feeling? Is the baby making you tired?"

Evangeline delicately blotted at her mouth with a napkin as if the close brush with the sugary treats had been enough to sully the perfect line of her lipstick. "The smell of the live-stock turns my stomach, but I've never been fond of animals anyway." She gave a delicate little sniff. "And I haven't managed a full night's sleep since I arrived. I hear Carlos coming out of his bedroom at all hours to check on that dirty horse and foal."

Sra Ana tried her level best to keep her features pleasant and even. "It is a working ranch and horse stud, my dear, and

Carlos is an equine vet. What did you say you were doing in Kentucky when you met?"

"My father owns some racehorses and we were down for the Derby." Clearly not allowing herself to be distracted, Evangeline continued her rant. "Anyway, I don't understand why he chose to be one. There is so much more money in small animals and you get better clientele as well."

Sra Ana didn't point out that Carlos's family were his clientele as an equine vet. She wasn't quite sure if the other woman was oblivious to the slight or didn't care if she insulted the family of her baby's father. Sra Ana suspected it was the latter. She bit down on her cookie, trying to find a neutral topic.

"Have you decided which doctor you are going to use for the baby's birth? I hear they are all good, but one in particular is very popular. I can find out his name from Deb if you like?"

Evangeline's lip curled before it was hidden behind her hand, an insincere giggle bubbling out. "Oh, you are funny, Ana." She shook her head condescendingly. "Oh. You were serious? Oh, goodness me, no. I won't be having the baby here." More derisive twitter escaped. "Can you imagine me having a baby in this backward dirty place? No, I will be returning home to The Hamptons. Mommy has already organized it for me."

Sra Ana looked down into her coffee mug that she held fast in white-knuckled hands, amazed that it hadn't shattered in her grip. She wondered what sort of woman her son had, by sharing a baby with, brought into the family. She greatly feared she already knew the answer. Her face devoid of her inner thoughts, she smiled placidly at Evangeline.

"Whatever you think is best, dear."

CHAPTER 13

Megan sat on the floor of the tack room, the contents of the ranch's foaling kit laid out before her. It seemed like overkill considering they now had a residential vet, but she liked to be prepared. At the end of the day, she didn't want to rely on Carlos. One at a time, she returned the items, making notes of what needed to be replaced and desperately trying not to think about him. It's not like he was sitting around thinking about her.

Placing the last bottle of disinfectant back into the kit, she shut the lid tight and stood up. She groaned in relief as she stretched out her back muscles.

"Um, am I interrupting?" Chloe peered in nervously. Although Megan had apologized, the young woman was still uncertain when she might trigger another episode. Megan sighed. Just another thing she'd messed up.

"Nope, all done here." She gave Chloe her friendliest smile. "What can I do for you?"

"I have a real quick question about something that's been bugging me."

"Fire away."

"Well, we mainly bed the horses down in shavings, but in the stalls we've been getting ready for the broodmares, we're using straw. Why?" Chloe rubbed her elbow self-consciously. "It's just that I'm new to all of this and I want to learn and know why we do stuff."

Megan felt humbled that, given the history between them, Chloe had still chosen to come to her. It made her more determined to mend the bridge she had burned down. "If everything goes well with foaling, the mares will be happiest if we let them give birth in the fields and, just to make our jobs that little bit more interesting, they mainly like to do it at night. But—and this is a big but—when things go pear-shaped, we need to have somewhere well-lit where we can provide care for them. That's why we're getting the foaling stalls ready. Wood shavings are fine for older horses, but with foals, the chunks of shaving can end up in their noses and other places we don't want. Plus, straw has better insulation, so they're nice and toasty when they have their little naps."

Chloe nodded, her face thoughtful. "That makes a lot of sense. I have a lot to learn from you." She gave a little jerk of her head in the direction of outside. "Well I'd better get back to it."

"Hey, Chloe?"

The other woman hesitated. "Yeah?"

"If you ever have a question about something, I'm more than happy to share what I know."

"Thanks, Megan." Chloe's whole face lit up with enthusiasm. "There's so much I want to learn—from you about the stud side of things, Deb with running a barn, and Frankie with training. I think my head would explode if I asked Gabi about running a business."

Megan laughed in agreement. "Yeah, there's a lot going on in that little brain of hers." Long after Chloe left, Megan turned the conversation over in her mind, mystified at the respect in the other woman's voice when she had admitted to wanting to learn from her.

∾

THE RED MARE WAS RESTLESS, the ligaments over her pelvis and under her tail drooped, giving her hindquarters a saggy appearance. Megan ran her hand lightly over Rosie's flank. "Easy, girl, let me just have a little peek under here." She peered at the mare's udder, noticing the colostrum dripping from the teats. "Well," she muttered. "Bloody well, indeed. I think we might have a foal here very soon if I'm not mistaken." Rosie returned to rearranging the straw bedding in her stall as if in agreement.

"How's my number one patient?" Megan hated herself for the way her heart leapt painfully at Carlos's voice.

"I think we'll have a foal today or, at the very latest, tomorrow morning." She kept her eyes focused on the horse making another lap of the stall, her sides distended.

"I'll go get the foaling alarm then." Megan was a little surprised at his easy acceptance of her statement, as if he trusted her judgement on the matter.

"You don't have to bother with that. I just have this feeling. I can't put my finger on it exactly, but I'll feel better if I sit up with her." Megan decided she couldn't hide behind the mare any longer and finally made her way over to the stall door to exit, Carlos stepping aside to allow her.

His eyes sparkled with his respect and admiration for her commitment to the mare. "I guess I'm in charge of the coffee then."

"You better bloody believe it," Megan sassed. "I'm going to grab a few things from home and then be right back."

"I'll be here."

Megan wasn't sure if she was pleased or not at his words. Either way, it didn't matter. She was doing this because Rosie needed her, and if her belly did a funny little flip flop, well it was best not to dwell on that.

MEGAN HAD FORGOTTEN the certain type of energy that came from sitting up watching a mare begin the journey that, God willing, would end in the miracle of life. Earlier, she had stacked and organized straw bales to give her a raised platform outside of Rosie's stall. Add some horse rugs for padding and a few blankets for warmth and she had a comfy nest to wait out the delivery.

Bright light spilled out into the dimly lit aisle, briefly illuminating the area before the closing door extinguished it. The aroma of fresh coffee tickled her nostrils, wafting from the mugs in Carlos's hands.

"I thought you might be in need of some sustenance," he said, carefully carrying his precious cargo as he climbed onto her straw platform. Megan, bundled up in her blankets, scooted over to make room for him.

"I came prepared." She pointed to a thermos beside her.

In the dim light, she could see his teeth gleaming white. "I should've known. Well, more for me I guess."

"It'd be a shame to waste it." Megan reached out her hand.

"I wouldn't want to force freshly brewed coffee on you, especially when you have hours-old thermos coffee. What sort of monster would I be if I did that?" He shuddered in mock horror at the thought.

"Just hand over the bloody coffee already," Megan said, her hand still out expectantly. Grinning, he finally relinquished the mug into her possession and settled in comfortably beside her. Megan tried not to notice the warmth coming from his body as she sipped her drink and watched Rosie swing her head agitatedly to her rippling side. "Poor Mommy," she murmured. As if to spite herself, she couldn't resist adding. "Speaking of mommies, where's your baby mama? I haven't seen her around today."

Carlos remained staring at the laboring mare, his face in profile to Megan. "She's back at her parents for some appointments." He turned to look at her. "Megan, how I feel about you—that hasn't changed." He let out a breath in frustration. "It would be so much easier if it had."

"Easier for who? You?" Megan bunched up the blanket in her fist. "From where I'm sitting, it wouldn't change anything for me."

"I'm sorry. That came out wrong."

"You think?"

"I don't care about Evangeline, not in the way I care about you. I don't think I will ever feel for her what I feel in my heart for you, Megan." He reached out a hand in the dim light, capturing hers in his warm grasp.

In the split second before his touch, every nerve in her body was electrified and Megan hated herself for feeling that way. "We could go around in circles about this for a long time. But it really doesn't bloody matter anymore, does it? It doesn't matter how you feel about me. All it comes down to is that Evangeline is the soon-to-be mother of your child, whether you planned it or not, and that's never bloody going to change."

How could she ever make him understand the hollow feeling she felt inside, like a black hole that sucked all the joy from her being? The anger she felt at herself for allowing herself to fall for him, for letting herself believe that, after watching her friends find their soulmates one by one, it was finally her turn.

Rosie let out a grunt as she stood to her feet. She raised

her tail and let out a small amount of urine. Megan leapt to her feet in alarm. "Carlos, did you see that?" She pointed to the red, velvety structure at the mare's vulva.

"I wish I hadn't." Carlos also leapt to his feet, bounding off the straw bales. "Looks like she's having a red bag delivery. If we can't get the placenta open in time and the foal's nose free, it won't get enough oxygen and won't survive."

The mare continued to strain, oblivious to the drama surrounding her. Megan grabbed her halter and spoke soothingly as Carlos began to scissor open the placenta. Suddenly, a great gush of fluids flooded onto the stall floor, splashing on the vet as he exposed the foal's nose and cleared the mucus from it. "It's breathing." Relief swamped his voice. "And I can see two front hooves."

"When you've finished checking, I'm going to start walking her around."

"Good idea. We need to get her to stop straining for a moment, otherwise it'll impact the foal in the birth canal."

As soon as Carlos stepped clear, Megan pulled the reluctant mare forward. "Come on, Rosie. I promise we only need to do a few laps to help settle a couple of things down and then I swear we'll leave you in peace to finish having your baby." The laboring mare let out a long groan as another contraction rippled through her.

Carlos kept a steady eye on the pair's progress. After a few moments, he spoke again. "Megan, I think we can let her be now."

As soon as Megan exited the stall, Rosie lay down on her side and began to push in earnest. Within minutes, the dark, wet, gleaming body of the foal lay on the trampled straw bedding. Rosie turned to inspect her newborn, nickering gently in greeting as she began to lick him from the tip of his fuzzy ears to his rump.

"I think we have a little colt on our hands," Megan whispered, overcome with the gratitude that always filled her with a successful live birth.

"I think you're right. Do you know what he's going to be called?"

"Probably something fancy when they register him, but I think we should call him Chance." Megan looked at Carlos, seeking his approval.

He smiled. "I like it. But he still isn't out of the woods yet. He's going to be on medication for a while yet, so I guess you could say he has a fighting chance now."

As he spoke, the little colt unfolded his spidery legs and wobblily attempted to stand. Rosie's enthusiastic licking sent the foal tumbling to the straw in a sprawled heap. Megan smiled encouragingly as the youngster tried again, this time successfully. He stood, trembling legs splayed as his dam urged him to her udder. Finally, after supreme effort, he made his way to the milk bar and his fuzzy tail pumped as he began to nurse.

"I think they're both going to be okay and I'll check on them every hour or so, just to be safe," Carlos promised. "You look exhausted. You should get some rest."

"You don't look that bloody crash hot yourself." Megan had to admit that wasn't entirely true. Even with fluids splashed over him, straw stuck to his clothing, and exhaustion stamped on his features, he was frustratingly still incredibly sexy.

"Megan, I—" His hand half reached for her before he pulled it back to his side, his heart in his eyes.

Megan gently stroked his cheek, a world of regret and sorrow buffeting her. "I know. And now we need to let it go." Before her will could desert her, she walked away.

CHAPTER 14

*A*fter Chance's arrival, it was as if the flood gates were thrown open and the foaling season began in earnest. Amongst the late-night checks, foaling alarms ringing, and the joy of new life, Megan was in her element. Carlos was now a constant presence as he checked on each new arrival and examined the mares yet to foal. With Evangeline still in The Hamptons, Megan allowed herself to enjoy his company. She was surprised to discover a genuine friendship growing between them, something deeper than the spark of physical attraction.

That's not to say her heart didn't flip flop whenever he turned toward her, laughing, his eyes sparkling with mirth as they shared a joke or the look of intense commitment as he battled to help a mare with a foal in distress. It was just now that she felt a level of connection she never had with anyone else before. It would have scared her if they were together—the intensity of the bond they would have had. But now, with the hand fate had dealt them, it simply filled her with sadness at what would never be.

"What are you taking to Vegas?" Chloe asked from the

floor where she was engaged in a very competitive tower building competition with Grace.

"Snacks, toys, diapers. Hopefully, Gracie figures out potty training soon and I can say goodbye to them," Deb replied from the kitchen where she was preparing dinner.

"Oh, yeah. I mean, obviously you would be taking those. I was meaning more like clothes." Chloe looked toward Megan. "What about you?"

She shrugged. "Clothes?"

Chloe rolled her eyes. "Yes, but what sort of clothes, exactly?"

Megan looked at her doubtfully, unsure what answer the other woman was searching for. "Clean clothes?"

"Seriously, you guys are no help." Chloe gave a groan as her tower toppled, prompting Grace to knock hers over as well.

Megan glanced at Deb. "Do you have any idea at all what she wants to know?"

Deb shook her head. "None. But I have an idea, let me try it." She looked down to where her giggling daughter was now playing peekaboo with the source of their confusion. "What are you taking, Chloe?"

"That's just the thing," Chloe wailed, bobbing her head up from behind her hands. "I have nothing to wear."

Deb dropped her head in her hands. "I swear I can't do this again. Last time almost broke me. I can't handle another Frankie."

Megan rose to sympathetically pat her friend on the shoulder. "It's okay. It'll be okay."

"What have I done to deserve this? I'm a good person," Deb sobbed.

"You are," comforted Megan. "But we all have our trials to bear and this, apparently, is yours."

"I literally have no idea what you two are talking about,"

Chloe complained from the floor. "But I suspect you're both trying to be funny."

Deb raised her head sharply. "I'll have you know I'm bloody hysterical." She turned to Megan. "You tell her."

"Um, well." Megan searched for the right words. "I guess you could be? You do have your moments that are almost … amusing."

"Thanks."

Megan patted Deb on the back. "Always here for you, mate."

"THANKS." Carlos accepted the cold beer from Joao. "You have no idea how much I need this."

Joao watched as he drained the drink. "I take it family life is not treating you so well?"

"Soon-to-be family life," Carlos corrected. "And no. All Evangeline does is complain about how dirty and backward it is here and why can't I get into a small animal practice? Why do I always smell like horses? Why haven't I bought her more gifts? Why don't I take her out to eat at fancy places? And that's when she's here. Which is never. At the smallest excuse, she jumps on a plane back to what she calls civilization." He was surprised to find his beer gone and put the bottle down, disappointed.

"Well, maybe it is the hormones?" Joao handed him a replacement.

"I wish. She was pretty high maintenance before, but now"—Carlos pinched the bridge of his nose—"now she's next level." He took another gulp of beer. "Man, I think I've made a mistake."

"Which bit?"

"All of it. We shouldn't be having this baby and that's the

only reason we ever got back together and Megan and I, well…" He paused to drink again. "Every time I see her, there's something between us and it's real. And the worst part is knowing I hurt her."

"But you are having this baby," Joao pointed out.

"Thank you very much, Captain Obvious." Carlos glared at his friend. "And there's no way I'm going to have a kid of mine raised without their dad."

"But if you are not happy with the mother?"

"Then I need to man up and deal with it." Carlos glanced down at another empty bottle. "Pass another, will you?"

MEGAN SLIPPED the lead rope around the little colt's rump causing him to dance in excitement. "Easy, Chance. It's going to be a long walk to the paddock if you keep this up." She nodded to Chloe who held Rosie. "Lead the way." Chloe swung the door open and began to lead the mare out. Chance began to bounce like a rubber ball.

"I'm glad I made it back in time to see this. He looks a bit excited for his big day. I'm going to miss my favorite patient."

A smile lit Megan's face brightly as she looked up, only to disappear at the sight of Carlos standing with Evangeline in front of their apartment stairs. "Yeah, he's a bit of a bloody handful right now."

Evangeline laid a proprietary hand on Carlos's arm. "Darling, I am feeling a bit tired after my trip. Do you think you can help me inside?" The look she sent Megan was pure cattiness. Frankly, it made Megan throw up a little in her mouth, the insipid little voice she spoke in.

Carlos looked down as if he just remembered that Evangeline was still there. "Of course, but after that, I need to head over and catch up with Gabi. She wants me to fill in some records for her."

Chance began to bounce again, eager to explore the great outdoors for the first time. Even Rosie tugged on the lead in Chloe's hand, keen for fresh grass after weeks of confinement. As Megan followed Rosie out, she couldn't help but see Evangeline pout up at Carlos. "But darling, can't that wait?"

Carlos laughed. "You have met my sister, right?"

"Well, she needs to learn that you have a family now and she can't expect you to run every time she snaps her fingers."

Megan's eyebrows shot up at the comment. *Yeah, right. That's bloody going to go down like a lead balloon with Gabi.* Carlos stepped out from Evangeline's touch.

"She asked me to do this a week ago—when I had a spare moment."

As she led the high-spirited foal outside after his mother, Megan wondered at the frustration she had heard in Carlos's voice. *Maybe all is not well in paradise after all.*

egan checked her watch. *Okay, five more minutes and I need to head back to the bunkhouse and start packing.* She looked at the colt frolicking around his mother. *I guess I can spare ten minutes.* There was a definite nip in the air and Megan was thankful for her coat as she stood watching Chance. The foal was as curious as a kitten, inquisitively checking out anything and everything that caught his attention. Megan smiled. It was hard to feel bitter when there was something so joyous about his antics. Maybe she should just swear off men and stick to the horses. At least they didn't leave her feeling all twisted up in knots inside.

A shadow fell over her. She squinted up to see Evangeline's pregnant outline silhouetted against the sun. *Yep, there goes that happy feeling.* "Hello, Evangeline. How are you feeling today?"

The pregnant woman peered down her well-bred nose as she looked her over. Her lip curled dismissively as if she didn't quite approve of what she saw. Megan had to force herself to not drop her eyes as if she wasn't worthy to keep direct eye contact. Evangeline gave a contemptuous sniff.

"I never did understand what he saw in you. Maybe after being with someone of my standing, he just wanted a piece of rough. Although, having met his family, maybe you reminded him of them."

For a moment, Megan couldn't quite believe her ears. It was one thing to insult her—people had been doing that her entire life—but to do it to the Cabrera's, that wasn't acceptable. "Thank you."

"I wouldn't thank me. I wasn't complimenting you."

"You might not have set out to do it, but I'd bloody take being compared to Carlos's family any day of the week. They are some of the best people I have ever met." Megan's eyes drilled into Evangeline's ice-blue ones.

Evangeline brushed at her spotless sleeve as if even standing this close to Megan could somehow make her dirty. "I really don't care what you think about them. What I care about is you staying away from Carlos."

"I'm the stud manager, and he's the vet for this ranch. We're going to have some sort of contact while undertaking our duties."

Evangeline thrust her belly out as she looked scornfully at her nemesis. "Megan, I'm not blind and you shouldn't make the mistake of thinking I'm stupid. I see the way you fawn over Carlos. He's too nice to say anything, but he finds it embarrassing. Everyone thinks it's pitiful." Megan's heart constricted painfully, humiliation making her eyes burn painfully. Her tormentor twisted the knife. "Seriously, I don't understand how you thought you even stood a chance with Carlos anyway. Why would he want a dirty, uneducated, poor little stable hand when he can be with me? My family is one of the wealthiest in the country. The mere mention of their name opens doors to some of the most exclusive clubs and houses in the world." Evangeline shook her head mockingly as she took in Megan's shattered expression. "Oh dear, you really believed he wanted you. Even if I wasn't carrying his baby, it was only a matter of time before I snapped my fingers and he would have come running back, tired of his little toy."

Megan wanted to roar her denial, make the smug rich girl take back her words. But how could she when, inside her head, the voice whispered its agreement? *Silly little Megan, that's what everyone was thinking as they laughed behind my back the whole time.*

She was so caught up in her inner torment that she almost missed Evangeline's final thrust at her heart. "I think it's best you hear all of this now. You are listening aren't you, Megan? By the end of our time in Las Vegas, Carlos will have proposed to me and I will not tolerate you being anywhere near him. Are we clear?"

Megan wasn't even sure if she nodded or not. But she must have done something as, appearing satisfied that she had made her point, Evangeline gave her one final dismissive look and departed. Megan stood motionless, no longer aware of her once joyful surroundings, the color having been sucked from the landscape around her.

"So, should I take the distressed denim or the blue denim jeans?" Chloe held up the apparel in question. "And while we're at it, are you taking that cute little gold belt of yours, Megan? Earth to Megan?"

Megan pulled her attention away from the fascinating piece of wall she had been morosely staring at. "I'm sorry, what?"

Chloe waggled the jeans at her. "Which one? And you said you would pack your gold belt so I could borrow it."

"You can take it. I've decided I'm not going."

Chloe blinked. "Ahh, say what?"

Deb walked into the lounge, trailing another suitcase behind her. "I swear Gracie is taking more with her than all of us combined." She looked at Chloe, jeans in hand. "Aren't you packed yet?"

"I am. Well, almost. But did you know Megan isn't going?" She threw Deb an accusing glare as if she had been holding a secret.

Deb's brows furrowed. "Don't be silly. Of course she's bloody going. Right, Megan?"

"I'm not going."

Deb crossed her arms as she looked at her friend in worried confusion. "All I have heard since the American is how you weren't missing out on the finals in Las Vegas and now you're not going? I don't get it."

"I don't want to leave Chance. He still needs someone to check on him and I wouldn't feel right leaving." Megan returned her attention to the wall.

Deb took in her depression and turned to Chloe. "Pack both of them and get a wiggle on. Now, shoo." She waited for the other woman to leave before taking a seat beside Megan. "You want to tell me what's really going on?"

"I told you. I don't want to leave Chance."

"Megan, I've known you a long time, and I love you dearly. And I know you're dedicated where the stud is concerned, but I don't think that's the real reason why you're staying here. Now, spill."

"I don't think I can stomach Evangeline gloating as I watch the man I love propose to her." Megan had been expecting some sort of relief to have actually uttered the words in her heart. Instead, she just felt emotionally exhausted.

"Megs, I don't think he's ever going to bloody propose to her."

"I'm tired, Deb. I've tried being friends with him, and I can, to a point. But having to watch the two of them together, it just bloody hurts too much. And then when the baby comes, I just don't think I can do it."

Deb put an arm around her friend. "Megan, it's so bloody unfair what happened."

"I'm not even bitter or angry anymore." Deb looked at Megan in askance at her words. Megan gave a hollow little laugh. "Yeah, I know. It surprised me, too. I'm just sad and tired of life a bit."

Deb gave her shoulders a squeeze. "You know, I really don't feel like packing any more bags, and all those bright lights on the strip make Gracie a bit hyper. Honestly, I'm getting too old for yard glasses of daiquiris and angry drivers beeping their horns every time I try to cross the road. I think we might stay home, too."

Megan shook her head in protest. "No, you don't have to do that. Go, have a good time. I'll be fine."

Her friend pulled her in close. "I remember once telling everyone I was okay. Never once did you leave me, and I have no intention of leaving you now."

"Frankie will miss you being there to support her."

"You're just as bloody important to me as Frankie. Anyway, she'll have more than enough people to cheer her on."

Megan gave a little sigh of acceptance. "We can always livestream it."

Deb smiled. "We can, indeed."

Frankie sat at the table beside Luciano, the line of fans waiting to greet her almost as long as his. She gave a pleased little smile as she remembered back to how it had been when they last sat here together. In her mind, she could almost see a little cowgirl all in pink determinedly dragging her father over to meet her. This year, as the number one contender to win the world championship, her name was a much bigger draw card.

With a quick flourish, she signed the poster in front of her and leaned in to get the requisite selfie. Knowing that she couldn't put off a bathroom visit any longer, she excused herself with the promise she would be back in five minutes. Frankie was rather impressed with how graciously the fan next in line accepted the interruption. Standing, she stretched her shoulders. "Luc, I have to quickly duck to the loo."

He gave her his megawatt smile that, even after nearly four years of marriage, still did funny things to her belly. "Do not be too long, Querida. I think your line is only going to get longer."

"It's tough being popular." Frankie tossed her hair, pretending to be a movie star. She bent down and gave him a quick kiss before briskly walking toward her destination.

As Frankie quickly checked her clothing was still in place in preparation for departing the bathroom, a flash of pale blonde hair caught her attention and she was surprised to see Evangeline making her way out of a cubicle. "Hi, Evangeline. I didn't know you were here checking out Cowboy Christmas. What do you think?"

Evangeline finished washing her hands and checked her makeup and hair fastidiously. "I can't say I care much for it, but Carlos was adamant that we come."

Frankie looked awkwardly at her, caught by surprise at the blunt reply. As they both exited the bathroom at the same time, she was expecting they would talk a little more. But as soon as Evangeline cleared the door, she headed off in her own direction without the need to further acknowledge Frankie's presence. "Okay, then. Looks like that's a goodbye. What a rude cow," she muttered under her breath.

Suddenly, Evangeline's progress halted, and her head jerked sharply to one side. She quickly changed her path and scurried off in the opposite direction, her head bent low. Curious, Frankie craned her neck to see what caused the dramatic change. She could see a man wearing slacks and a jacket, staring in the direction Evangeline had just departed, his expression hard.

Frankie pondered the scenario she had just witnessed as she made her way back to Luciano. Something very fishy was going on and she was going to find out what.

THE COOL AIR burned Megan's throat with each breath she sucked in, her muscles on fire as she pushed her body onward. If she could just run fast enough, far enough, maybe she could escape this feeling that she was doomed, always to be life's trash, discarded broken once she was no longer of use. Everyone here, they had a purpose, but she had always just drifted where the currents took her, too scared to want anything too much in case it was snatched away from her again. Maybe that was why she was being punished now? She had dared to dream, had wanted things to be better for herself. Limbs trembling, she turned for home, knowing what she had to do.

"I THOUGHT I'd find you out here," Deb said, joining Megan in leaning on the fence rail. "He looks good." She gestured to the little bay colt.

Megan smiled. "Yeah, he's a tough little thing, but I think he's going to be okay." She continued to stare out into the paddock. "I'm going back home."

"To the bunkhouse?"

"No, Australia."

"I don't understand. What about Chance?"

Megan turned to face her friend. "I know you and Chloe will look after him, and you're wrong. I do need to do this. I—I need to do something, at least, and this is all I can think of to do."

"What about us? We're family. Sure, it's a bit of a mixed bag, but it's still a family." Deb's voice was rough with emotion.

"You guys are more my family than my own ever was. But I just can't stay here anymore. Maybe when it's not all so raw —when it doesn't hurt so much—I can come back. But for now, I need some space and time to distance myself from it all." Megan didn't know how to find the words, that she had liked the person she was around Carlos, that somehow, when she looked at herself through his eyes, she had seemed worthwhile, not bitter and used up. That she was desperately clinging to that image and she was scared, so scared, that she would start believing the voice in her head again. A voice that had started to sound like Evangeline.

Deb's expression clouded. "You can't leave me. Who'll laugh at my jokes?"

"I never laughed at your bloody jokes." Megan shook her head vigorously in denial.

"Sure, you did."

"Seriously, I never found your bloody jokes funny."

Deb smiled sadly. "I guess I should start planning your farewell party. When are you thinking of leaving?"

"Tomorrow."

Deb's mouth dropped open in shock. "You can't be serious. You're leaving without saying goodbye to the girls, to Frankie?"

Megan crossed her arms defensively across her chest. "By the end of Vegas, Frankie will be World Champ. She won't even notice I'm gone."

"Megan, that's where you're wrong. Frankie loves you. She's going to be heartbroken to come home and find that you've left for good and not even said goodbye. What about the Cabrera's? I know you care about them. Don't you think they at least deserve a farewell?"

Abruptly, Megan stepped away from her friend, deciding she had had enough of the conversation. "I need to start packing."

CHAPTER 17

Frankie's round had been nothing short of amazing, Sampson had tried his heart out again for her and left nothing in the tank. She was still buzzing from being the night's winner and leading the points race for the world championship gold buckle. Hurrying back from settling Sampson in his stall and desperate to make it back in time to see Luciano ride, Frankie almost missed Evangeline standing partially hidden behind some vendor boxes. In fact, she wouldn't have notice her at all if it wasn't for the sole reason that the usually icy calm blonde was gesturing extravagantly while she was speaking.

Frankie stopped dead in her tracks when she realized that the man talking agitatedly to Evangeline was the same man that had freaked her out earlier. Frankie stood, indecisively chewing her lip as she pondered what to do. Seriously, she did not want to intrude where she wasn't welcome—especially when she wanted to see her husband compete. But at the same time, Evangeline was pregnant, and the honorable part of her couldn't stand it if the other woman was being hassled. Heaving a sigh and knowing that she was probably going to regret it, she changed course and headed over.

"Hey, Evangeline," Frankie called out, noting curiously that the conversation ceased the minute both parties became aware they were no longer alone. "I think only competitors are meant to be in this part of the stadium. Are you lost?" She stared curiously at the man. If there was ever someone that didn't look like they belonged at a rodeo, it was this guy. His clothes were designer and looked better suited to heading to a country club.

"Hello, Frankie." Evangeline sounded strained, her words tightly clipped. "I hadn't realized that I had wondered so far from the main area. I'm a bit embarrassed to say I got lost and I was just asking this gentleman for help." She held herself so rigid that Frankie was surprised her lungs had room to breathe.

Frankie turned innocent eyes to the man. "What company are you here with?"

The man gave her a hard look, his eyes dead as they stared back at her. "I'm not here on business." He returned his reptilian gaze back to Evangeline. "I'm sure your friend will be able to help you find your way back. I'm sure I'll see you around again before this is all over." Frankie wasn't sure if it was a threat or a promise but, judging by Evangeline's naturally alabaster skin turning even paler, she definitely interpreted it as menacing.

Frankie waited till the man had departed before turning to the pregnant woman. "I don't know what that was"—she gestured between where the man had stood and Evangeline —"but if you're in some sort of trouble, you should tell Carlos."

Evangeline turned frigid eyes to her, her expression so hostile Frankie took a step back trying to put some distance between them. Seeing Frankie's obvious apprehension, Evangeline attempted to smile. "I'm not sure I know what you mean. I had a silly moment and got lost. The man I asked for help was a little strange, but I just assumed he was like you and part of the rodeo."

Frankie felt like she was in some sort of strange movie, the words not matching the scene she had witnessed. She shivered, suddenly feeling extremely uncomfortable being alone with Evangeline. "Um, I need to get back to see Luc ride." She silently chastised herself for being silly as she hurried away, but that didn't make the hairs on the back of her neck settle down.

WHEN SHE WAS LITTLE, sometimes Megan's mom would need a little break. Then she would be dumped at some relative's place or, worse, a foster home, with a garbage bag full of her possessions and left for however long it was going to be that time. As she stood looking at the contents of her life, once again ready to be packed up, the harsh memories of her childhood swam to the surface. How was it that her entire life fitted in two suitcases with room to spare?

Grace noisily entered the bedroom, crumbs coating her mouth and most of the front of her shirt. "Hello, Gracie. I see you've found some cookies." Megan greeted the little intruder.

Grace held out a hand that contained a half-eaten chocolate chip cookie and offered it to Megan. "Won fwor, Mwegan."

Mitch laughed from the doorway as Megan took the sugary treat from the adorable youngster. "She found the stash that Sra Ana left for us." Guiltily, he took a bite from the cookie he had been hiding behind his back. "I might not have saved any for Deb."

Megan laughed. "I'm glad I'm not in your shoes when she finds out. You know how much she loves Sra Ana's cooking —almost as much as Frankie's." A stab of sorrow hit hard at the thought that she would soon be leaving all this behind.

It must have shown on her face as Mitch smiled sadly at her. "You know you don't have to do this."

"I need to." She looked down at Grace trying to climb into one of her suitcases. "Gracie, I'd love to take you with me, but I think Mommy and Daddy would miss you. And what about Senhor and Sra Cabrera?" Megan's voice choked as a wave of loss crashed into her.

"Mwiss Mwegan, too." The little girl said earnestly, toppling out of the bag and coming over to give Megan a hug.

"No fair." Megan looked up at Mitch accusingly. "You're bloody playing dirty and using Grace to make me feel bad."

Mitch smiled at her. "Whatever we need to do to get you to stay."

Megan wrapped an arm around the little girl who had nestled into her lap. "This is bloody hard enough as it is. I need to know that you understand why I'm doing this."

He scratched his neck thoughtfully. "I might not agree with it, but I respect that it's something you need to do. I just want you to know that if you ever need to come back home to us, you call me, or any of us, and we'll move heaven and earth to get you back here. Okay?"

His face blurred in front of Megan as tears pooled. She nodded as they spilled down her face, the little girl warm and comforting in her arms.

～

"I SWEAR TO GOD, if one of you guys don't answer your phones, I'm never bloody speaking to you again," Deb threatened as Gabi's phone rang out. She mashed in the same message she had sent to Frankie and Chloe's phones moment earlier. Frustrated, she held her phone to her forehead and closed her eyes. *Please guys, I need you.*

CHAPTER 18

Frankie nestled in close to Luciano as they both celebrated their round wins after their appearance on stage at Southpoint to accept their buckles. One would anticipate that, surrounded as she was by her loved ones, she would have been in a euphoric bubble. But instead, a thorn of unease threatened to pop it. Frankie cast a baleful look of resentment across at the source. Evangeline cozied up to Carlos, clinging to him like a limpet, all while he looked glumly about.

"Querida, I am secure in your love, but if I was less so, I would think I had to worry about the attention you are paying Carlos."

Frankie looked guiltily up at her husband, remorseful that she had spoiled his enjoyment of the evening. "Babe, I have my hands full with you. No way I'm eyeing someone off. Well, not like that at least, but I don't trust Evangeline." She proceeded to fill him in on what she had seen earlier.

Luciano listened gravely, his glance flicking from time to time in Evangeline's direction, but otherwise intently following her words. Once she had finished, he nodded, his eyes troubled. "I think we need to tell Carlos what you have seen."

Frankie chewed her lip, suddenly less certain now that she had voiced her unease aloud. "I mean, I don't want to cause any trouble."

"And what if you are right and something is going on? Would you let Carlos marry a woman like that?"

Her spine stiffened with determination. "Well, when you put it like that… But I don't want to go over there while she's around."

Her husband smiled in understanding. "Then we wait until we see our opportunity, and then we pounce."

In the end, it happened surprisingly easily. The woman was, after all, pregnant, and before long, left in search of a bathroom. "Now," whispered Luciano urgently in Frankie's ear and, dragging her behind him, he powered over to Carlos.

The man in question looked rather surprised at the determined pair boring down on him. "Um, hi, guys. Congratulations on your wins again."

"Thank you, it was a good night for both of us. I was happy to get the eight seconds on Buttercup." Frankie tugged on Luc's hand, returning his attention to why they had come over. "Ah." He cleared his throat. "Frankie has something she needs to tell you."

Carlos looked curiously at Frankie. Although he knew her, he had not spent as much time with her as the other girls since she had been on the road fairly consistently since his arrival. "Sure, Frankie. What can I help you with?"

Frankie wet her lips, suddenly anxious that she had made a big issue out of nothing. "Um, well, it's just that I've seen a man hanging around and he seems pretty interested in Evangeline. But she seems pretty keen to avoid him."

Carlos shrugged. "Maybe it's someone that she used to know and doesn't like?"

"I thought the same. But then I saw them talking together in a pretty out of the way place. She seemed pretty upset about it and, when I went over to see if she was okay, she said she didn't know him. But I would bet anything they did."

Frankie couldn't interpret Carlos's expression. She wasn't sure she had adequately summed up exactly how strange the meeting had been. What happened if she couldn't make him understand? Finally, he nodded.

"Thank you for letting me know about this. I'll bring it up with Evangeline and make sure everything is okay. I'm sure it is. Now, if you'll excuse me, I think it's my turn to buy Papai a drink."

Frankie turned to Luc in amazement. "He doesn't seem to care at all."

"That is not entirely true. He said he would talk to her about it."

"We need to find that man!"

Luciano gave a little groan. "I was afraid you would say that, my Querida. But I think you are right." He gave a sweeping gesture. "Lead the way."

"OH, CARLOS, YOU STARTLED ME." Evangeline held her hand to her heart, her eyes wide. She gave a nervous laugh. "It's sweet of you to follow me, but I'm sure you don't have to stand guard outside of the ladies' bathroom."

Carlos looked at her closely. Her laughter seemed forced, her voice a little too breathless. "Is everything all right, Evangeline?"

Her eyes were guileless. "Of course. Why wouldn't they be?"

The certainty that she was lying to him hit him hard in the gut. "Frankie said that a man has been hassling you."

Again, that breathless little laugh, her hand dismissively gesturing as if shooing a fly. "I'm afraid that Frankie misinterpreted what she saw. I did try to explain to her that I was merely asking for directions, but she simply had it in her head that I must have known him."

Carlos held his gaze steady. "So you're saying you've never met him before?"

"Never." She smiled, her eyes shining her innocence a little too brightly, before dropping her gaze.

The mistrust settled into a hard ball. "Then Frankie must have been mistaken, as you said."

"I wasn't." Frankie's voice rang out loudly.

"Frankie, be a dear and just let it go already. You made a mistake, but this is beginning to become a bit of a joke, don't you think?" Evangeline said, her voice dripping in patronization.

"I thought you might say something like that, so I brought proof." Carlos turned sharply at Frankie's words to see her gesture and, moments later, Luciano stepped out of the shadows with a man firmly in his grip. At his side, Evangeline gave a little gasp, her expression horrified, before smoothing out to its usual blandness. "Everyone, meet Stirling. Or should I say Carlos, meet Stirling, since he and Evangeline already know each other. And boy, has he got a story to tell." Frankie's eyes gleamed wickedly with anticipation.

"Honestly, darling, we don't have to listen to any of this." Evangeline tried to pull Carlos away. He jerked his arm free of her grasping hold.

"Oh, I think I might." Carlos nodded at the stranger, inexplicably numb to what was about to unfold. "How do you know each other, exactly?"

"Carlos, please." Evangeline latched on again.

"Let the man speak!" he roared, goaded into angry action at her incessant prattle.

Stirling gave the pregnant woman a satisfied smirk. "I know her because she was my brother's girlfriend or, should I say, my married brother's mistress." He smiled smugly at the furious glare Evangeline threw at him. "But she disappeared for a while once she got pregnant and my brother refused to leave his wife. But she didn't stay away for long. It didn't take her long to start coming around again, telling him that she forgave him and she had found a way that they could still be together."

"Is this true?" Carlos's voice was deathly quiet, the quick flash of anger burnt out, reduced now to something much deadlier—a coldly simmering fury. The fury that only a man that had been made to look like a fool could feel.

"Carlos, darling, he is obviously lying." Evangeline's hand trembled on his arm, despite her bravado. "I think we should leave."

"How long were you with that man? Were you seeing him when we were together?" Horrified, he looked at her with sudden clarity. "Is the baby even mine?"

"Carlos, I—" Her hand crept to her throat, fussing with the pearls that hung there.

"Is. It. Mine?" Carlos's jaw was locked so tightly the words were ground out from between his clenched teeth.

"No." The words were so quiet she could have breathed them.

He leaned forward, he face inches from hers. "Say it again."

"No." Evangeline raised her tear-stained face to his, wrapping her arms around her swollen belly. "What was I meant to do? You've met my family. Even having you as the father was better than—"

"Being pregnant with the child of a married man?" Carlos could barely breathe over the fury that fought with the grief of the loss of a child he had thought was his. "How could you do that to me? Were you two sleeping together while we were still a couple?" He could see the answer in her eyes, eyes that he had once thought so beautiful but now he saw what he should have seen from the start. They were as cold as her heart. "I left the woman I was falling in love with—I gave her up to do the honorable thing. Turns out there was nothing honorable about it at all."

Evangeline clutched at his arm desperately. "But what am I going to do?"

He looked down at her in disgust. "I really don't care. Actually, that's not true. There's something I care about, and that's never seeing you again." As he walked away, underneath the pain of her betrayal and the loss of the child he had thought was his swam relief. The relief that he was free of her for good.

CHAPTER 19

The phone buzzed incessantly in Frankie's pocket. No longer in the thick of the Evangeline drama, she finally had the luxury to answer it. She was surprised to see Deb had been the one that had been blowing up her phone. "Oh, my goodness, Deb." She flicked her hair out of her face. "Whatever it is, you have nothing on what's just happened here."

"Really? Megan has packed up all her things and, in a few hours, will be leaving the country … for good."

Frankie's stomach dropped at the unexpected news. "What do you mean? What happened?"

"What do you think happened? There was no way she could stay around with what happened. Could you?"

"About that. It's not a problem anymore."

There was a pause on the other end of the phone. "What do you mean not anymore?"

"Long story, but Evangeline is a big fat liar and Carlos is through with her." Frankie said with a great deal of relish.

"Well, he better hurry and make his mind up about Megan before it's too late."

"I'm on it." Frankie quickly hung up her phone and bolted, urgency thrumming through her body as she desperately sought the ranch's vet, all the while praying she would find him in time.

IT WAS BITTERSWEET. The sense of having dodged a bullet, a bullet named Evangeline. Carlos gave a wry smile as he brought the bottle slowly to his lips. Nothing like beer to wash away the sour taste of betrayal. What an idiot he'd been. At the end, before they had broken up, he'd suspected that she had been sneaking around with someone else, but once she'd turned up pregnant on his doorstep, he never imagined that the baby was anyone else's but his. And he had been so determined to do the honorable thing, noble in his suffering as he pined for the woman that he had fallen in love with and now could no longer have. What an idiot!

"Carlos, oh my goodness, I'm bloody glad I found you. I hope there's still time." Frankie's words tumbled over themselves, spilling out in a torrent.

He raised bleary eyes to meet hers. "I don't really care too much about the concept of time right now. I have always felt that it was nothing more than a temporary relationship between events. Although, I believe Buddha believed that time only existed in our process of knowing."

Frankie's face went blank with confusion before she rapidly blinked it away. "I literally have no bloody idea what you just said, but you need to hurry." She tugged at his arm but, to her dismay, found him as immovable as a rock. "You need to bloody well move."

"I don't really have any place and anywhere I need to be. Not anymore." He took another casual sip of his beer.

Frankie stared at him, her expression frustrated. "Don't you think you're overdoing this a bit?"

"No."

"Fine, well I guess Megan can always send you a postcard when she gets settled back in Australia."

His hand froze, the bottle inches from his mouth. "What did you say?"

"What I've been trying to say the whole time, but you were too busy playing the role of uncaring man of the world. Megan has packed up and is on her way to the airport to fly back home to Australia. Permanently."

"Not on my watch she isn't." Carlos slammed the bottle hard on the table, beer splashing out onto the counter. "Why didn't you lead with that instead of wasting my time discussing philosophy?"

Frankie spluttered indignantly. "You did not just try to blame me." She shook her head, determination etched on her face. "I'm not going to let you sidetrack me. If you want to be with Megan, you need to make your mind up. But I suggest you don't dawdle too long or you might lose her and, this time, you might never see her again."

Without another word, he stood and fled the bar.

"GRACIE, this is as far as we're allowed to go with Auntie Megan." Deb looked on sadly as her daughter clung to Megan's hand, unwilling to let go.

"Noooo!" Grace wailed. "Auntie Megan has to stay." Her face scrunched up, about to explode into a full, epic meltdown.

Megan knelt beside the little girl, envious that she was able to express her emotions so vividly. "Gracie, I wish I could stay, but I have to go. One day, I don't know when, but I promise I will come back."

"No!" Grace stamped her foot angrily. "That's not twue! You don't want to stay, you don't wove me."

Megan's heart broke beneath Gracie's words. *Better I go while she still wants me to love her. One day, she'll turn away like everyone else.* She wrapped the upset girl in her arms and squeezed her tight. "I love you, Gracie, and don't ever believe anything else." She stood, her eyes misty, and turned to give Deb her farewells. "Well, we had a good run while it lasted."

Deb wiped her damp eyes. "Yeah, I mean there were a few moments I wanted to give you a kick for being a cow, but mainly, I'm glad you were here on this adventure with us. It's not going to be the bloody same without you."

Megan shrugged modestly. "What can I say? I'd like to think that I've left my mark."

"You certainly did. Thank you for everything you did for me and Gracie." Deb bravely sniffled back her tears. "Better give me a hug before I lose it." She threw her arms around her much smaller friend. "You ever need anything—and I mean anything—you give me a call. You give any of us a call and we'll be there. You promise me, Megan."

Megan's throat was thick with unshed tears. "I promise, Deb. Thanks for always being my friend, even when I wasn't the easiest person to be around." She took a deep, shaky breath. "Okay, I'd better get going while I still can. She looked at mother and daughter through blurry eyes. "I love you guys. I'll send a message when I land." She walked determinedly toward the customs gate, scared she would weaken if she stayed any longer.

MEGAN HAD NEVER NOTICED before how truly depressing

airport lounges were. The color scheme was designed to be as unstimulating as possible. Best not let the unwashed masses get too excited before boarding their aircraft to destinations unknown. She looked down at the unread magazine that lay open on her lap. *How did I get here? Did I think it was ever going to end up any way other than me being alone?*

Megan had felt bleakness in her life, but this black hole of despair robbed her of breath. She had met Deb and Frankie when they were preteens and they had been a family ever since. She'd spent so much time over at Frankie's house growing up that she used to pretend it was her home, her family. Deb must have felt the same since she was always there, too. For the first time since she had met those two girls, she was about to be truly alone. Her mind shuddered away from the thought. Surely, focusing on that was courting madness. Every fiber in her being fought against her leaving, screaming out that it was wrong.

A commotion drew her attention to the security gate. The guards appeared to be attempting to restrain someone. The dark-haired man was waving his arm about, yelling something she couldn't quite make out. She leaned forward, curious as to what was going on.

"Megan!"

Her head jerked. Surely, he wasn't calling her name. She rose to her feet. *What on earth is going on?*

"Megan!" It couldn't be. She took a few tentative steps. "Megan, please, I need to speak to you. Let me go. I just need to talk to her for a few moments." Carlos wrestled with the guards, a battle that he was slowly losing.

"Carlos, what are you doing here?" She was incredulous at the sight of him.

"Please, can you just come out here for a minute? These jokers won't let me in because I haven't got a ticket." He threw a filthy look at the security personnel that were attempting to subdue him.

Suddenly uncomfortably conscious at the curious stares of her fellow travelers, she collected her bag and hurried away from their gaze. "It's okay, I'll make sure he doesn't cause any more trouble," she promised as she walked back through the checkpoint. Carlos threw them one final dirty look and followed—nay, strutted—after her. Once clear, she turned, hands on her hips. "Now, do you want to tell me what all of this is about?"

"You can't leave."

Her heart pounded painfully in her chest. "I understand why we can't be together, but it's killing me to watch you with Evangeline. And if it hurts this much now, how will I handle it when the baby arrives?"

"There's no baby." Bitterness laced every word as his eyes burned with something akin to hatred.

"What? But she's very obviously pregnant." Megan's face scrunched up as she tilted her head in confusion.

"Well, there's a baby, but it's not mine. The only reason I ever let you go was because I thought it was the right thing to do for my child. Now, I've been given a second chance and, if you will allow me, I can't imagine my life without you in it. Please, don't go."

Megan watched as his beautiful ebony eyes pleaded, begging her to stay. "I never wanted to, but I was lost as to where I belonged."

His eyes burned into hers with an intensity that threatened to set her soul on fire as he took her in his arms. "This is where you belong, right here, forever. I love you." The words were so simple that it belied the complexity of the emotions it triggered in Megan.

"I love you too, and since you're the first guy I've said that to since I was nineteen, that's something. But maybe next time, try to be a little less bloody dramatic."

"Does that mean you'll stay?"

"Since my heart is here, I think I should."

He lowered his head and kissed her, his lips laying claim to what was his. In his arms, the voice that had controlled Megan's sense of worth for so long was silenced once and for all. At long last, Megan knew what she deserved, and it was to be in the arms of the man that loved her.

Megan stood, her mind at peace, anchored by Carlos's loving arm draped around her. For the first time ever, she felt like she truly belonged to a place, to a family—not one that was pretend. These were her people, and she would never run away from them again. Over the last few years, they had grown from young girls with stars in their eyes. It seemed like another lifetime ago when three Aussie girls had dared dream that one of them would someday be the world champion. And somehow, against all odds, they had managed it. Frankie wore the gold world champion barrel racing buckle at her slender waist.

Megan smiled, proud that she had, in her own way, helped secure it for her. There was a lightness to her soul that she had only achieved once she learned the hardest lesson of all. She needed to value herself, to love herself. And once she had done that, she had been able to let go of all the pain and hurt from her childhood and the anger and bitterness she had carried with her into adulthood.

Senhor Eduardo, beaming, gestured for quiet. "My family, tonight we celebrate another world champion to our numbers. Frankie, I knew when I saw you that you had the fire of a champion in your belly. Even if you did worry more than any person I have ever met. Sra Ana and I are so very proud of you." His voice choked and he raised his glass. "To Frankie, our world champion."

"To Frankie," the crowd responded enthusiastically.

"Speech, speech!" called Deb.

Frankie gave her a dirty look as she was ushered to the front. "This is a dream that only came true because of the support of the people I love, all of whom are here tonight." She looked nervously at Luciano and he sent her a reassuring smile. "Luc and I have decided that, over the next few years, we will transition from competing full time to enjoying life at home and maybe start having some little champions of our own, if only to give Senhor Eduardo something to do in his retirement. " Everyone laughed. Senhor Eduardo and Sra Ana looked vastly pleased with her statement.

"I'm already in negotiations with Bryce over their future sponsorship deals," called Gabi. Chuckles greeted her words. "It's probably why he couldn't make it here tonight to help celebrate with his newest champion, but at least the bourbon's safe."

Frankie smiled modestly. "Now, back to what I was saying. To do that, we have decided that we will begin work on setting up our ranch as the training facility for Affinity Ranch. We plan on building a world class arena with accommodation to hold clinics. Of course, it will be in the capable hands of Gabi to project manage." Once again, laughter rang out.

"I have so many ideas," Gabi said, enthusiasm shining brightly on her face.

"Of course you do," Deb replied from where she held an exhausted Grace, the child almost on the brink of sleep. "The builders are still recovering from your slave driving with the vet complex.

"It should be easier for them now that they're used to me." Gabi waggled her finger in the air.

Carlos cleared his throat nervously. "Well, since everyone Megan and I love is here, I think it's the perfect time to do this. Hopefully, if Megan tries to run away again, there's enough of you to grab her before she gets too far."

Megan's heart fluttered in her chest, her pulse increasing when he dropped to one knee. "I could tell you pretty words about what you mean to me and they would all be true, but what really matters is that I knew your worth the moment I saw you, that your heart was beautiful and true. I almost lost that, and I thank God every day I was lucky enough to have a second chance. Believe me, I'm not stupid enough to risk losing you again. Megan Gehler, will you marry me?"

"Yes." Megan's knees went weak, slowly giving way till she dropped down to her knees, joining him on the ground. Her heart, so recently mended, felt like it would shatter all over again, this time from the love that overflowed it. She valiantly blinked back tears, trying to see his beloved face. "Yes. There's no one else I could ever imagine saying that to."

Their family cheered and hollered out their congratulations as Carlos leaned in and kissed her soundly. In the night sky overhead, a shooting star burned brightly across space before flickering out, its beauty too perfect to have ever been meant to last long, and all was right with the world.

THROUGH THE KITCHEN WINDOW, Megan could see Chance frolicking beside his mother, sending butterflies fluttering into the crisp spring morning. The usually placid mare, driven to distraction by her high-spirited offspring, finally walked away, seeking solitude. Megan smiled at the scene, feeling a sense of connection with the animals.

"Such a pretty smile to be greeted by," Carlos said, returning from a late night dealing with a neighbor's elderly pony that had colic. Although he specialized almost solely in working with equine reproduction and sport horse management these days, when the call had come through, he hadn't hesitated to go. It was just another reason she loved her handsome husband.

"I don't think I've ever smiled as much in my life as I have since I married you." Megan tilted her head to accept a loving kiss from Carlos. "You make me happy."

His eyes smoldered as he reached for her. "I can think of better ways to make you happy than standing in front of the kitchen sink, woman."

Megan laughed as his lips tickled the tender skin at the nape of her neck. She fended him away with a tea towel. "Is that an offer for you to do them?"

"We had a deal, remember? I cook, you do the dishes. Anyway, you have mail."

He handed an official looking envelope to her. A quick glance at the logo on it told her it was from the veterinarian college she had applied to. She sucked on the inside of her cheek, gently tracing the edge of the paper with her fingertip.

"Well? Are you going to open it and put me out of my suspense?" Carlos demanded.

She smiled cheekily at him as she slowly opened it, all the while maintaining steady eye contact with him, enjoying tormenting him as he impatiently looked on. She looked at the official words, the print harsh against the white background.

"Well?" prompted her husband.

Pure, unadulterated satisfaction filled her to her core. "It says they would like to offer me a position in their upcoming semester." She barely got the words out before she was caught in a giant bear hug, the breath whooshing from her lungs. She laughed giddily at his excitement, enjoying the pride and happiness her achievement had brought. Once he finally calmed down, she took a deep breath, uncertainty furrowing her brow. "I think I'll defer for a year."

Carlos's eyes opened wide in disbelief at her words. "Why on earth would you want to do that?" Sudden comprehension dawned across his face. "Is it nerves? Don't worry about that. We all get them when we first start, but you're so ready for this."

Megan had to smile at his unconditional support, it was something that she was still getting used to and never wanted to take for granted. "I love you so much."

"I love you, too."

"I promise I'll return to college after the year off, but there's something I need to do first."

"What?"

"Have your baby."

It was like watching the sun come out from behind the clouds. A smile lit across Carlos's face, his dimples dancing. "Baby?"

"Yes." Her answering smile was just as joyous. "It appears that we are about to have another generation of Cabrera's."

"I hope you like soup."

"Soup?"

"Mae is going to feed you so much soup you're going to pop." His eyes twinkled mischievously.

Megan laughed, memories flooding back. "That's right. I'd forgotten your mae used to bring it to Deb—and lots of other stuff, if I remember correctly."

Carlos walked closer, capturing her hand to pull her into his loving arms. "Well, now it's your turn, Mrs Cabrera. I didn't think I could love you anymore, but this"—he reverently touched his hand to her stomach—"this. We're going to have a baby, Megan." Wonderment filled his voice.

A warmth flowed through her body as Megan finally realized that she was enough, that she was loved. At last, she could allow herself to feel a cowgirl's pride.

THE END

As an Indie Author, reviews help me get my books noticed. If you enjoyed reading Megan's story as much as I did writing it, please leave a review, it will make all the difference to me

If you loved, *A Cowgirl's Pride,* sign up for my newsletter at https://www.edithmackenzie-author.com to get updates on new releases as well as exclusive extras.

Now, turn the page as the Affinity Stud Ranch story continues with Chloe...

A COWGIRL'S LOVE SNEAK PEEK

Chloe stared at the picture of the bull staring back at her, trust Travis to have that as his profile picture. She could imagine him sitting down at a battered old desk, scrolling through the pictures on his phone, trying to decide which bull picture he liked best. She giggled a little at the thought as she quickly typed in a message and attached the pictures of a growing Nova. Teeny was still too young to have her own account, so Chloe sent everything about the young horse via her father. Not that she had a problem with that at all. In fact, it gave her the perfect excuse to stay in regular contact with him.

"You almost finished?" Deb tried to look over the pretty young blonde's shoulder.

Chloe quickly hit send, not before realizing she'd made several errors. *He's going to think a fifth grader sent it.* Giving a little groan, she turned to face her friend. "You know it's rude to read over someone's shoulder."

"Oh, was it personal?" Deb's eyes were wide in feigned innocence. She popped a piece of gum into her mouth.

"No, I was just sending some pics of Nova to Teeny." Chloe held her hand out for Deb to share.

Handing the packet over, Deb's eyes sparkled impishly. "Oh, so it was personal then. You were sending a message to Travis." She made a kissing face as she said his name.

Chloe could feel her face heat up as the blood rushed to the surface. She was about to deny it when Gabi, Frankie and Megan entered the bunkhouse. *Dang it. I forgot we had a meeting this morning.*

"Talking about Travis again?" Megan asked as she settled herself into her customary chair.

"What makes you think we're talking about Travis?" Chloe asked, giving the chuckling Deb a dark look.

"Well, you only ever get that particular shade of red when you're either talking about or to Travis." Gabi winked at the others, as she placed her laptop on the table.

"Are you going to help, Frankie?" Chloe pleaded, mortified at the conversation that swirled around her.

Frankie laid a sympathetic hand on her shoulder. Gratitude that someone was finally going to put a stop to this discussion flashed through her and she sent a smug look to the others. "Welcome to the club, kiddo. All I can say is, it'll be painful. And they have a lot of experience and stamina as far as teasing about this particular subject. Stay strong and, eventually, they'll lose interest. Either that, or you'll get used to it."

Chloe looked up, shocked at her idol's betrayal. "That's it?"

"That's it." Frankie calmly sat down. "Now, what's on the agenda for today's meeting?

ACKNOWLEDGMENTS

The usual thanks to my editor Rebekah Groves for her patience with me, even when she has exciting things happening in her own career. I would like that I hired an editor, but gained a friend.

Another big thanks to Megan from Designed with Grace for her cover design.

My beta reader Teri Hermans, your attention to detail and love of the characters give me so much joy and the inspiration to continue with their stories.

A cowgirl's movie star

A fiery cowgirl with big dreams. A movie star far from home. When their two worlds collide, will their love be strong enough to hold them together or will they be pulled apart

A cowgirl's billionaire

Release Dec 2020

Christmas Standalone Books

Boots and Mistletoe

ABOUT THE AUTHOR

Edith MacKenzie or Eddie Mac to her friends is an author of sweet and wholesome contemporary cowboy romance. They say in literary circles to write what you know, and Eddie has certainly taken that to heart. Before embarking on a writing career, she trained horses professionally and brings that wealth of knowledge to her writing.

Now a mom to a boy and girl, as well as wife, she delights with her tales of strong cowgirls and their adventures in finding love. When not weaving the love stories of her characters, she enjoys hanging out with her family and animals, as well as reading, fishing and camping

Just remember once a cowgirl, always a cowgirl.

facebook.com/EddieMacAuthor
bookbub.com/profile/edith-mackenzie
amazon.com/Edith-MacKenzie
instagram.com/edith_mackenzie_author

A GLOSSARY OF AUSSIE SLANG

Now everyone knows that cobbers from the Land Down Under speak the Queen's English, but if you don't know to Tracky Daks from your Servo, I've put together a quick little cheat sheet.

A few stubbies short of a six pack - Crazy

Ankle Bitter - Small child

Arvo - Afternoon

Blind - Intoxicated

Bloody - Very. Used to extenuate a point

Bloody oath - Yes or its true

Bludger - Someone who is lazy

Buggered - Exhausted

Cark it - Die

Choccy Bikkie - Chocolate cookie

Clucky - Feeling maternal

Crook - Feeling sick

Daks - Trousers e.g. Tracky Daks are tracksuit pants

Dog's breakfast - Messy (does not relate to food), a bit of a shambles

Dry as a dead dingo's doing - Exceptionally dry

Flat out like a lizard drinking' - Not doing very much at all

Grog - Alcohol

Hit the frog and toad - Hit the road, get going

Man's not a camel - A man gets thirsty and would indeed like the beverage you are offering him

Mate - Friend or conversely could be someone you barely know

Nay, Yeah - Yes

Pull the wool over someone's eyes - To trick or mislead someone

Reckon - For sure

Ripsnorter - Can also be interchanged with beaut, bonza. Someone doing something exceptionally good

Servo - Petrol Station

Six one way, half a dozen the other - Undecided

Sparrow Fart - Before the crack of dawn. Very, very early in the morning

Stone the flamin' crow - An utterance of surprise of annoyance

Struth - God's truth. Used to express surprise or dismay

She'll be right - Everything is going to okay

Tell 'em they're dreaming - Is never in a million years going to happen

Tighter than a fish's bum - Said person is very frugal with their money

To blow smoke up someone's bum - To give praise that might make the other person cocky or overly confident

Up yourself - Stuck up

Ute - Pickup Truck

Whoop whoop - Middle of nowhere

Wrap ya laughing gear 'round that - Eat this

Yarn - To talk or tell tall tales

Yeah, nay - No

You bloody ripper - Very good, a job well done

www.ingramcontent.com/pod-product-compliance
Lightning Source LLC
Chambersburg PA
CBHW021203110726

47900CB00002B/712